BLACK BOOK CHRONICLES: VOL 1

The Year of Aphesis

Order this book online at www.trafford.com
or email orders@trafford.com

Most Trafford titles are also available at major online book retailers.

Note for Librarians: A cataloguing record for this book is available from Library
and Archives Canada at www.collectionscanada.ca/amicus/index-e.html

Printed in Victoria, BC, Canada.

ISBN: 978-1-4269-1604-5 (sc)

*Our mission is to efficiently provide the world's finest, most comprehensive book publishing
service, enabling every author to experience success. To find out how to publish your book, your
way, and have it available worldwide, visit us online at www.trafford.com*

Trafford rev. 10/09/2009

 www.trafford.com

North America & international
toll-free: 1 888 232 4444 (USA & Canada)
phone: 250 383 6864 ✦ fax: 812 355 4082

DEDICATIONS

I have to dedicate this one to My Mother and Father, my "Mary and Joseph", because they were both there and still are. I Love both of you for teaching me how to be a Man. Life is short and shouldn't be taken for granted. People come and people go; it's the release of the soul. That's why we have to teach the youth how to "love to live". We should also cherish and value the moments that we have with them. Our days are numbered, but our memories can be everlasting.

Also to the Virgin Saints, Sons of God, and members of the Divine Seven. Peace comes among us. Let's get back to the movement and start standing up for what we believe. Stop allowing our words and thoughts to be oppressed by their ideas and theories.

This one also goes out to all the young and old school players that are trying to keep the game going. Don't ever give up on the GAME. And also to all the haters, without you, there is no me. Thank you for bringing me out of ME.

And most importantly To my brothers: our walk through childhood was great, now we have the duty of guiding the youth in this corrupted world. To my little ones: Berta, Kayla, And Buddy. Uncle Chai will always love you for being you. Grow strong with knowledge and claim your place on God's Earth. Don't ever run from a challenge, for it then becomes your handicap. Be loyal to our family and protect future generations through knowledge and wisdom. Learn to live by the basic laws for they will guide each of you. This story was told not for the story itself but the message that lies within. Be at peace with yourself and peace will be unto you.

ACKNOWLEDGEMENTS

I would first like to start BY THANKING GOD for showing Me the way THEN MY MOTHER AND FATHER for keeping me safe, and MY BROTHERS WHO taught me how to REACT, THINK, and live the meaning of CARPE DIEM.

THEN, my FAMILY THAT ALWAYS STOOD by me and made sure I kept my head UP. TO ALL MY FALLEN HoMIES, We're ALWAYS going to be CREW TIGHT. To Mario, Artess, Antonio, Kwane, Coach Al and all the other fallen soldiers, Watch after the CREW. Bless us in this time of need.

To My Past for walking with ME: Smash, Dre, Lil Chancy. AND TO ALL MY HOOD HoMIES who watched me cross over. Stay true to the CAUSE. To THE CREW Smooth, Hack, Bat, Too, Ham, Cake, Tra. To the BIRDGANG, JGutter, Q, Niq, Mo, Swoops. Vaughn 3. Keep grinding every DAY and NIGHT. 50 deep at the HIGH, 2G1. And for the real walls that never told. Stone, Cook, Fie'it Up Ent. From MIAMI to D.C., coast to coast, SEA to SEA: REAL Soldiers know me. To my literary teachers Rena, Gheri, and Mrs. Watkins and My sister in faith, Brandy. Thank you for helping me. Bless You.

THEN TO ALL MY READERS, ENJOY THE STORY AS IF IT were true, but I'M not going to SAY that IT IS, because it wouldn't be WISE . . . if I DO.

"My presence is my testimony." Anyone with eyes to see should read to understand. History is repeated.

A REAL KING WALKS . . .

TABLE OF CONTENTS

Prologue

WELCOME TO MY LIFE

Loyalty

THE phone dropped and hit the floor. All the pieces went separate ways. I didn't want to put it back together because the
thought of it ringing again scared me. My headed felt heavy. My
body was tired. My feet were hurting.

I sat there on the edge of my bed with my safe open. I was looking at my way out. "Could this me the end of me?" I thought to
myself. I closed the safe and got all of those awful thoughts out of
my head. I jumped up and yelled, "Aaaaaahhhhhh". Everything was
falling apart. It was a deep cut that bled for months. To tell you the
truth, it was my fault.

I had to pack my bags, I was going home again. The night had
lost all life. The air was still. The loyalty for my heart was lost. I
had to start thinking logically now. Each moment that brought
me to this day and time was flashing before my eyes. My gaze was
thick but clear. The blinds were closed and the windows were shut
tight in my dorm room. Nothing was moving.

My books covered my desk, and there were so many dirty
clothes in my closet that the door wouldn't close. We were going

into the last game of the season but I had nothing to do with the team anymore. Things just weren't going the way I planned.

I stood in front of my dresser throwing meaningless articles of clothing into my duffle bag . . . socks, underwear . . . it didn't matter. Everything had to go. I paused to think.

I had messed up. I wasn't myself. This wasn't how I was raised. I was becoming someone else. In this short time away from home I had become my own caricature.

I walked back and forth pacing the floor as if that were going to solve my problems. I stopped and looked in the mirror at the foot of my bed. By now, I was talking to myself. First, in a calm tone then eventually cursing myself out to the point where I wasn't talking to myself anymore.

I was going crazy by now. I couldn't even bear to look at myself. As I stepped on my first college research papers, the anger grew. I got a "D" on it. I could have done a lot better but I was out the night before getting drunk. I know I finished it at the last minute. I probably had to get an extension knowing me.

For the most part, I was just playing the game. I had become obsessed with the game: hanging out, getting drunk, and sleeping with many females. That's what I did. Well, not anymore.

I stopped packing my bags for a moment and threw some noodles in the microwave. I hadn't eaten all day, and I was starting to feel a little dazed. I stretched out on the bed while I was waiting for them to finish cooking. I wanted to just fall asleep. I still strained to close my eyes, blocking out the thought of what had happened.

I thought about every possible way of turning things around. I opened my eyes as the microwave went off. I looked at the clock; it was 3:59 a.m. I had to get out of here.

There was no one in the hallway as I put my first bag down outside the door. The entire hallway was quiet. Everyone was sleeping, studying, or having "random relations"—as my grandmother would say. I had to think for a moment and start at the beginning. Did it matter? I had to ask myself, "What for?"

I leaned on my bed and put my chin on my chest. I could hear a million voices screaming in my head. Everyone was talking to me, all at the same time. I couldn't answer everyone. My mind was spinning, and my eyes were doing the same motion.

I wasn't ready to leave this campus and go home. I hated to be judged by the people who loved me. The thought alone was the worst pain in the world, totally unendurable.

My mind was at peace in this position. I had my legs crossed, and my arms were at rest on the bed. My bed was waist high because of my bed-lifts. At first, I thought bed-lifts were for females, but once I saw how small the dorms were it became obvious why people used them. Plus, it put the bed at the right height for everything else.

Royalty

I placed another bag outside my door. My sigh was endless, and I began to think that only the walls could feel my pain. The walls were the only ones that had seen what happened and had to have heard all the lies told. I knew exactly what I was doing, but continued to act out. It was like I couldn't say "no" to myself.

It was going to be a nice ride back to the crib by myself. Five hours the hard way; by myself. I needed a moment of peace, giving myself a little time to think. I was going to have to drive slower than usual because it had started to snow a couple of hours ago. The seasons had changed just as my peers' shoulders.

The weather was crazy. Because we were in the mountains, the seasons changed daily. It was just the beginning of November, and we were seeing those bubble coats that people in the south wear when it gets to about sixty degrees outside. But it was like ten degrees up here.

I felt like just heading down the hall and chopping it up with the boys, but I knew that regardless of what I would say, the facts remained true. It was college, and I realized that everyone had their goals in life and were not stopping on account of me. They didn't know who I was anymore and sure didn't care what I was going to become. The notion grew pointless.

This was a prestigious, ivy-league University of the south. That meant that everything changed just as many times as the daily news came on. Everyone was money. I was just an example of having a strong support team.

Everyone supported me from the junkies to the winos, pimps to players, cops to teachers. I knew the man that delivered your mail all the way up to the man that delivered your baby: credence of hood law, seeing that my father was in and out of jail, and it was the responsibility of the community to raise me. The way it should be.

I was the second oldest of seven. I was respected. I never had to want for anything back home. I was royalty at the crib. Now I had the heavy burden on my shoulders of explaining why I couldn't make it on my own. I let everyone down. I let the royal family down. I was just another statistic.

The air had even smelled different on my campus. It was the perfect educational setting that every parent would dream of sending their child; I treated it like the ghetto that I had left behind to become somebody.

Honor

My university was in a city that was more laid back and easy going than what I was used to. A perfect place for me to stir up some stuff and get into trouble with my big-city mentally. Hanging out all night and acting like I had no parental advisement while growing up became my life.

I arrived on my college campus the day after graduation from high school. That summer of my freshmen year started off jumpin'. Everything was going great.

I wasn't too far away from home so I was on the first thing smoking as soon as I got my diploma. I was taking advantage of every moment and that seemed to make sense to me at the time. Then, for some reason, everything hit the fan.

I hated the fact that I messed everything up. I stood up straight, took a deep breath, and I still felt terrible on the inside. I couldn't shake it. I had forgotten about the noodles. I stood there in front of the microwave looking at the campus newspaper article about me.

It read "Freshmen To Watch". Under the title was a big picture of me. I was pouring some water on my face at practice. The caption read "Freshmen expected to see early action this season." That was before I had sprained my ankle.

The next day coach decided to red shirt me so I could " . . . focus on getting back healthy". I knew the real reason. The coaches and the alumni wanted Andrew Joe, a hometown All-American, to play. It was an acceptable political move, only mentally tolerable to me because I was injured.

I was the typical blue chip athlete coming out of high school. I worked out during the day and enjoyed myself at night. Parties, drugs, and money; this was the perfect situation for a guy like me. A city boy.

We weren't the richest family, but we were the richest in the hood. My mom worked two jobs and made sure my little brothers, sisters, and I got a good education.

Thinking back to even before I came to campus, while I was being recruited, the university showed me that I could be supported by females and drugs. Everything was money oriented. They showed me what life was like when you don't have to worry about how much something cost. The concept of money was eliminated and just the essential meat of the fruit was left for me to taste.

That was one of the main reasons I chose this school. Both football and females would keep me motivated and focused. College females wanted to have a fun time. That was the dream that was imbedded in me, and I pursued it: to live like a playboy, to achieve the American dream, being adored by women.

I was standing there sucking the life out of myself by this point. I had lost my honor. I had to get moving. I hit the radio and started moving to the beat. I had abused every moment of college like it was a cheap stripper. I saw a lot of promise in my new situation, but now it was a mere phase of my life that I wished I could have back.

The papers on my desk fell as I bumped my knee on it trying to grab my hat off the wall. I wasn't worried about Tina. It was my mom and what she would say. How was I going to tell her? I knew she was going to compare me to my father. It was going to become another period in my life where my mom and I would just look at each other. No words. I was back at the bottom of the Totem pole.

It was made perfectly clear that I was either going to college or joining the Army. I made that decision quick, put on some cleats, and put a ball in my hand. I played football more like it was a passion and not as though it was my potential profession.

I did everything growing up from karate to water polo, but football was the game that I loved. The other reason I came to this university was to play in one of the most competitive conferences in the nation. I was a trained Buffalo Soldier with the mentality of Geronimo. I was not the chief, but many depended on my intellect and wisdom to lead, and a real rebel when it came to war.

I became a territorial defender. I was trained not to allow anyone past me. I was a true warrior with deep scars and war wounds from the field of battle. Just a mere game, this thing called football was to me since I was seven years old. Now I was in the position wherein this dream could be fulfilled.

This ordeal made me realize that I was just like everyone else who had entered college looking for adventure and exploration. I was no different from any other freshmen. I was almost glad that certain things happened for me to learn about college; I learned early.

College forced me to grow up quickly. I remember my first year of high school, me and my boys had that entire year before we had to get serious. Here, they will get rid of you, just like they did me.

I threw all of my duffle bags over my shoulders as I headed towards the elevator. I left the door to my room open just in case anyone walked by they would know that I left. It was a floor rule.

Whenever anyone left the floor, they had to leave their door open so that way it could become another party room. I had three bags on my back, and I was dragging another that had all of my shoes in it. As I pressed the down button on the elevator, I could hear someone's television. The silence was broken.

College was like a new beginning for me. I learned that most students felt college was a place where any and everything that was wrong with their lives could be magically erased. Many tried to form new identities and new personalities.

I was even stupid enough to think that the freedom from parental oppression would relieve my stress. I didn't realize that the ridicule and depression I was going to experience was completely going to be of my own actions and decisions. This realization was not exclusive. Most freshmen feel like this.

Well, all of that didn't matter now, did it? My fine, athletic, and well-educated self was headed home. I knew where things went wrong. I knew I had to stop playing this game. I knew the difference between right and wrong, but yet and still I had allowed my stupid self to get into all kinds of trouble. And I knew the truth. The truth had to be told.

As I walked out of the lobby, I took one more look back at elevator doors closing as if I was exiting stage left and the drama play was over. I was the only one holding myself back from achieving greatness. I knew it. I had to change my thoughts, my ways, and my habits. I had to stop playing this game

Chapter I

SWAG CHECK

"When a story is told in a room, remember that everyone leaves with their own perception of what happened. Everyone has a different story to tell."

Whatz Happenin'

I GOT back to my dark cold room around two o'clock in the morning. I had left the air on earlier, and the sudden change in temperature stirred up my judgment. I tumbled and escaped a fall by catching myself on the corner of the dresser. I could feel my mind commanding my body but the lame specimen I had become was not responding. It became a losing battle in which I eventually gave up on as I fell face first onto the bed. My feet were tangled in a cable wire. I laid there.

My pants were bunched up around my ankles as I strugged to take them off. I kept forgetting my shoes were still on. I must have spilled something on my shirt because it was starting to stick to my chest as I rolled over and put my face into the pillow. I was drunk. I passed out.

I had to have been asleep for about twenty minutes before I looked up. "Whatz happenin?" I said, peeling my lips apart to figure out why Sarah was still here.

"You keep going to sleep," Sarah replied as I took a deep breath and released it like a whoopie cushion. "Get up ... get up," she kept saying, trying to command me. But I wasn't paying her any attention and didn't take commands from females very well anyway.

"Stop staring at me. That's so annoying," I said after I had cracked my eyes open several times, and she was still in the same position just looking at me.

I rolled over, turned my back, and faced the wall. She came and stood by the bed rubbing on my back. She was trying to convince me that she was more important than my sleep. I threw one leg on the wall and the other I let hang off the bed to let her know that there was no room for her. I was in my room, in my bed.

She gave me a little push in my back before she grabbed her bag. "I'm leaving," she said under her breath as if she was irritated by my actions.

"Thank You," I mumbled.

"Don't ever call me again," Sarah said snapping back as she walked out of the door.

"Ok, I'll call you tomorrow," I said as some slobber hit the pillow, forcing me to turn back over and switch positions to get comfortable again.

It was the second day of class and my second party this week. It was a Tuesday night, and I knew I had class as well as football practice in the morning, but I didn't care. That party was jumpin'. I had collected at least five new numbers in my pocket and another five that went straight into my phone. I mean females everywhere.

I had a lot to drink, but I wasn't drunk. I just needed Sarah to be my designated driver. She really thought she was going to stay over here, that was not going to happen.

It was still early in my eyes. It wasn't even three o'clock. The strip clubs were still open, they didn't close until four. If strip clubs are open that means that the night is not over. I was really trying to get a quick nap in and have Sarah in my room to wake me up. Goal accomplished.

I figured out some time ago, around the age of four, that attractive, charismatic people get away with a lot more devious things. So, I took that theory and ran with it. I have a lot of theories. The biggest one of my theories is my Theory of Life. Within the game of life, everyone is a player. Everyone. I think Shakespeare said something like that.

Within this game we call Life there are rules and responsibilities by which each member must play. Once you have mastered one stage of life you are accepted into the next phase. This is called maturity.

I knew about being responsible and all, but college was fun. I wanted to run around like a child on a playground.

Since I was too old to actually run around on a playground I used the football field to embarrass my peers in gladiator-like competition. It was almost like having a second life. I was a totally different type of beast on the field.

Football was my way of staying in shape. I wasn't out there for comradeship and sportsmanship. I was out there because females loved football just as much as I loved entertaining a crowd of over a hundred thousand. I loved it.

I cut on the TV and popped straight up. I had my energy back by now and was going through my phone again. The music channel was playing them explicit videos, and the lust for another body grew stronger.

Since summer football camp ended I was at every party every night: coming in late, missing class . . . the usual things that any freshmen would do. The only difference is that I was pushing it to the limit, seeing how far I could go. I really didn't care about anything. I was going hard like a defensive end coming off the edge.

I lay back down wondering if I should call someone with or without a car. I was not trying to leave again, so I began with the first available one with a car. By now, my pants and shoes were off, and I could put my feet on the bed. The room was dim; the only light came from the lamp on the desk and the light coming from my phone. I sat there in my football shorts with my number on them. I didn't feel like talking to anyone. That is when the text message game began.

I hit up a couple of new numbers and then a couple of old ones. I sent the same message to each and every last one of them, "Where U At?" I wasn't about any games. I just needed to know where they were, in order to make the proper decisions. First come, first served. I didn't need to know what she was doing because it was me. I was always top priority.

My phone started vibrating my leg, and I let the ring tone play out a little bit because it was kind of feeling good. Plus, it was just a message, it wasn't like anyone was waiting for me to pick up and talk.

"Where R U?" Someone replied back with the same text I sent.

I didn't reply at the moment. All that text meant was that she wanted to talk and not really trying to come see me. I laid back on the bed and placed the phone on my chest.

Then another text came. "U still ^? What R U Doing? IM still Out!!"

So I replied back, "Who is this, new phone" just to get a name, cause I didn't know who it could have been. I wasn't in a position to just be picking up or answering any text if I didn't know who it was.

"Jazz" the next text read. I had been waiting on this text for about a week now. I met Jazz last Friday, but didn't save her number to my phone. She knew where I stayed because her friend brought her over to play cards with us: like we were really playing cards, nothing but eye talking the whole night. We were communicating through winks and long intimate pauses.

I was ready for her, "Come thru" I texted back. "K" she replied to say she was on her way.

It's cute when girls text 'K', but if a guy does it then he is gay. OK. And men, stop saying "no-homo", cause I don't believe you.

My Roots

I was wild and had made a lot of bad decisions in my life, needless to say, but youth gave me an unbiased attitude towards the world. Everyone makes mistakes, so I made mine going a hundred miles per hour.

The things I've done these last couple of months could have gotten me locked up, shot at, or killed. But it was cool because I was at college. Honestly, I could look someone in their eyes and say, "I didn't know, I'm a freshman," and be perfectly cool with it. It was amusing to me. We were living in a bubble.

By this time, I had stripped down to my boxers and was doing a couple sets of push ups. It's always good to stretch and get some kind of cardio in before you play a game. I grabbed my towel off the back of the door and jogged down the hall to the shower area. A white boy was shaving in the mirror and had the best shower running as if he was about to get in.

"Thanks for running my water," I said as I jumped into the shower and closed the curtain. I could tell that he was mad, but I didn't care. He knew not to say anything. I was a two hundred and four pound corner back that ran a four-three on any surface. If that white boy looked at me wrong he knew I was going to make his life difficult.

"I'll be right out," I told him as he made a comment that he believed something was wrong with the shower head. He was lying to get me out of the shower. I did this on the usual basis.

One time I was so drunk I thought someone's bed was a towel and peed all over their sheets. They never knew who did it, and I sure wasn't about to tell on myself.

I was trying not to get my hair wet or it would be that way all night. My hair was like wool and came down to my shoulders. Each way I would wear my hair would reflect the mood I was in. It often changed three times a day. I would wear it up, down, in a

Mohawk, or pulled back depending on the situation. I hadn't cut my hair in three years and didn't plan on cutting it any time soon. My image was everything to me.

So when I'm in battle during the process of a game, I wear my hair loose and wild. It gives the image of a disturbed animal that reacts on pure instincts. I was enjoying every minute of life. Everything was being provided at will and all that was required of me was to train and entertain.

My days were endless. I was living three days, each day, and on the fourth day I would rest in order to finish the last three days of the week with the best. I know my parents intended for my college years to serve as a molding block. I was to find my individuality and my path in life.

My mom was a big advocate of education. She always stressed the fact of being knowledgeable in different situations. That's where I get my street smarts.

I mostly stayed with my grandparents because my mom was always working. Since my oldest brother was always gone with his Crew, my mother would have me collect money from all my uncles and say it was for a sports event or something. I loved my mother and did as I was told. In the process she was creating a beast, a young hustler.

I became the player that I am by watching my grandfather and the older men in my family. I possessed a unique swag and presidential style of charisma that the old heads respected. The ability to charm is power beyond belief. My words enchanted people. I appealed to just about every female that I interacted with. I learned early how to read between the lines and keep my mouth closed.

There was nothing wrong with my father growing up. He was just always gone. I knew my father was in and out of jail with all his court trouble. My mom would tell me that he was a businessman and always away on business, more like a hustler than a businessman.

Now, what I did get from my father was being humble. He didn't play any sports but he was a great player of the game called Life. He was intelligent in his decision making. What he said he meant, and he never really talked unless something needed to be said. He was a real gangsta in my eyes, in every aspect of the street life.

I was taught by my grandfather to never judge my father. I just knew what I had to do in order to make it, so I didn't need him. I said I was grown because I handled responsibilities not because of my age.

I found out the truth when I was seven. He was a player and had been for a long time. Everyone thought he was crazy, but he was one of the most intelligent people I knew. He was just too smart for his own good. He never thought he would be caught at what he was doing, which meant that he didn't watch his back like he should have. I liked when he would come home. We would sit around for hours and debate about everything that didn't make any sense.

Now my grandfather, Poppa Edwards is a whole different story in itself. My grandfather didn't believe in any American traditions like church, holidays, or marriage. He was never married to my grandmother.

He got married once a couple of years back but that was a joke. He married some twenty-two year old foreign exchange student. That lasted about two weeks.

I know he got paid out of the deal. Marriage was just a financial tie between families to Poppa: a way of preserving wealth within a family. He always had young women around him. Poppa Edwards has to be at least seventy-five.

Once Poppa Edwards found out I was going to college he started warning me about all types of crazy things like women in the night and Sorcery. He was also a big adversary when it came to pledging.

"To pledge means to submit, and I ain't bending over for nobody," he told me when I got the nerve to ask him should I join a fraternity on campus.

When my grandfather finally did decide to have a girlfriend last year, he had a ceremony as if it was a wedding. A girlfriend was a serious commitment for a man like himself. He even gave her a ring out of dedication purposes and everything. My grandfather was wild but remained loyal, and not only did he know how to play the game, he knew how to teach it also.

In fact, I knew he had many different families all over the South. My grandfather would always be gone for weeks and weeks, and my grandma would never say why. They had been together for eighty years and never been married. She was a loyal woman. She would just keep pushing on. I guess after years of being around a person you learn that people don't change. So if you truly love someone you have to understand that person's intentions and not just their goals. My grandfather always meant well. Their love was unconditional love.

My grandmother told me once that just having me around was good enough for her because we all looked just alike; my father, grandfather, and myself. My high cheek bones and broad shoulders were similar but I had a slight imprint of a dimple on my cheek that gave me a distinct look. "You are even cuter than the cutest man I know," she used to tell me.

Life was easy to me because I was easy on the eyes. She hated when I cut the two slashes in my eyebrows. She thought I was crazy.

The way I see it is, some time ago my people were enslaved. Ok. Let's get past that part. The part that everyone is missing is that only the strong survived. My great grandfather was the biggest and strongest slave, bred to be disciplined but dependent on others for mental stability.

So just imagine over time, as the great grandson of a chosen few of the strongest and wisest colored men, a seventh generation grandchild of Nat Turner. I was a living member of the Davidic bloodline. Imagine how my brain has evolved throughout centuries. Just look at Malcolm X's grandson. He is crazy, and it's kind of cool because of who his grandfather was.

Envisioning my passion was like visualizing four hundred years of oppression in a cub. Mine was like that same cub chained up and locked down at the zoo, waking each day having to fight the unbelievable and unimaginable goal of one day being physically free, till one day he gives up. Imagine being taught how to be helpless, not realizing that the cage has been lifted and now as a lion he is enslaved mentally.

Then, just as direct as the water hitting me in the face, I came to the realization that I wasn't any animal. I didn't have any chains holding me back from my exploration.

I was wide open and running as fast as I could. I was physically fit and mentally aware, waiting on any challenges. I was a young lion trapped within human flesh hoping to run wild again.

I cut the shower off. "Hey," the little white boy said as I jumped out and jogged back down the hall to my room. I always ran down the hall with my towel hanging half way off just in case a young lady was in the hallway and would care to take a look at what I had to offer.

"You could have left the water on!" I heard him yell down the hallway at me.

"You straight," I yelled back as I had already reached the end of the hall.

I had shoes everywhere, and my clothes were just thrown in the closet with no regard. Money was never a problem just because my father was always gone. One thing he did do was give my mother a couple of stacks each month to take me shopping. That's probably the reason she never filed for child support or anything like that. So, I do thank my father for keeping me fresher than any body else.

Being around all that money at that young age made me realize the opportunities that having money possesses. This also brought about my craving for women. Money! Women loved money! I knew that. So I always kept a lot of it on me.

I walked around with at least five hundred dollars on a regular day and at least one thousand dollars if I was going out. I didn't believe in asking anyone for money. Women can smell money and it IS the most attractive aspect of a real man.

As I threw on a wife-beater, I remembered when one girl tried to tell me that "money didn't matter to her". This was at the time when I didn't have that much. I knew that it is not the money that I had at the time, but the potential that brought about her attraction. All it takes is a single attraction to connect with a person. Whether it be love, hate, or indifference, you have a certain connection to that person. I was going to make a lot of money, and she knew it. Everyone knew it.

I had to move all of these brochures and club flyers out of my chair so I could sit at the desk and get my music right. I should've just thrown all of these flyers away when I got them.

I was being introduced to different career opportunities and numerous internships in order to gain financial stability, but all that was just to show on paper. I had to play the real paper game. I wanted to retire getting my money from females at this point in my life. If football didn't work I was going to become a certified pimp.

I was focused on the females and playing football. That was it. I was going to be finished with school in three years, and that's only because you have to play three years of college football to go Pro.

If it didn't have anything to do with football, it had nothing to do with me. I was straight.

In my initial meeting with my counselor, I should have been frank with her. I really didn't enjoy school or the idea of having someone lecture to me about something. I could care less. All I knew and cared about was football and females.

Hoe-ology was my major and Leadership was my track. I studied females: the way they acted, moved, talked, and socialized with others. I needed to know all of these things because I was sure it was going to be on the mid-term exam. With the females, it was almost too easy. Since my overbearing personality consumed theirs, I learned how to communicate nonverbally in order to preserve all of the extra talking. During every stage of my life, including high school, they also conformed to my whim.

Being a freshman again, having to adjust to a new environment was straight with me, but I could tell that many of my teammates had difficulty adjusting during their first summer away from home. Everyone seemed to have the, "I was the big man on my high school campus syndrome". I never won a state championship in high school but it seemed as if everyone on my team had, which made talking about our high school football days fun. Even though they had a state ring, they still couldn't beat me.

"IM Out>," Jazz texted me as I was putting on some lotion. This was a co-ed dorm so I didn't have to go downstairs and get her like at a Historic Black College.

"Come up," I sent back to her.

The freshmen were called all types names like "neo", "rook", or whatever came to mind by the upper classmen. But this was me. I had a new agenda for all these haters. It was a new mental challenge I had to direct in a positive way, a thinking game I might say. I saw college as a nice game of chess where my opponent has a slight advantage.

Everyone was from everywhere and lies hid behind smiles. I trusted no one, because I believe that trust will get you killed. Trust deals with one's ability, not his loyalty. You trust people with work not lives.

I had to realize that my place on the food chain had been reduced to the lower end, but being able to adjust in an atmosphere where people have mental control over what you do shows your true worth. I had to change up the game and switch my swag to charisma. I wasn't a kid anymore. I had this college thing on lock. I was not new to this at all.

Knock, Knock.

"It's open!"

College

"Get your lazy self up . . . See, that's what I'm talking about," Mickey said as he busted into my room.

I was no fan of the morning. It was still dark in the room. The door was open and the light from the hallway shined in like a watchtower. I couldn't see what time it was but had a good idea it was early because Mickey was up running around.

"Me and your mama pay all this money and you're lying in this bed doing nothing with your life . . . Get up Boi." Mickey and I were going to fight with him coming in my room with all this loud talking. Jazz must have left my door open when she left.

"Get out of my room."

I turned over and Mickey was sitting on the edge of my bed smiling. "And get off of my bed White Boi."

"Oh, so now it's a black thang," Mickey said standing up like he was LL or somebody.

Mickey was my suitemate, so our rooms were connected by the same bathroom. He was one of the richest of the rich kids here.

His father was a big time actor and comedian with over twenty box office hits.

Mickey knew how to have fun when it was time but was motivated to make his own money, which I commended him for. When we would be in the streets he would never say who his father was to get something. He was a real hustler, just a cool white boi.

I never had a hang-over before, so I couldn't tell if I was having one now. The only thing I knew was that my head was killing me. Sitting straight up on the bed made me realize that I couldn't stand up or walk so I laid back down for a minute. Last night was wild. My bed was removed a little off of the wall, and my pillow was filling the gap like loess. I was not ready to get up.

"Another night at the bars, I see," Mickey added to the conversation.

"I know you saw the first one I brought back." I couldn't remember anything about how she looked.

"Yeah, and what did you do to that one?" he asked with a concerned look on his face.

"I ain't did nothing to her. I don't think, why?" I had a concerned look by now with the feeling of bad news on my stomach.

"She ran out of here cursing and yelling down the hall. She was fine, too. Just point me in the direction of her dorm." Mickey was cool, he just talked too much. I was going back to sleep by now. I closed my eyes until I heard Mickey going in the refrigerator.

"What ya'll got to drink?" Mickey said as he reviewed what was on each shelf.

"Mickey?"

"Yeah?" he answered as if I was about to ask him a question.

"Leave." I fell back on to the bed and closed my eyes.

"OK, but remember you can't miss any more classes."

"Yeah, yeah" I said as I closed the door with my foot.

The room got quiet again. The only horizon I was expanding was my sexual horizon. I couldn't find the remote control so I just lay there. Time was passing. Bob Marley, Martin Luther King, and Muhammad Ali were all on the wall trying to tell me to get up, but I wasn't listening to them either.

It was almost too quiet in my room. I couldn't move. Every time I tried to move my head, I got dizzy. I laid back down four times before I actually fell out the bed and laid on the floor for awhile. I'd already missed my nine o'clock. I had to go to my ten o'clock; my football position coach usually would check that one. Plus, this class only met on Wednesdays, so I couldn't miss it or it would be like I missed the entire week. I began to use the noise coming from the construction next door for a rhythm. I was just being lazy at this point.

It felt like I was lying in quicksand. I jumped up at about ten o'clock, on the dot, threw on some sweats and ran out the door. My class was in the Vann Building, which was on the other side of campus. The professor never expected me to come early anyways.

I hit a little shortcut through this new freshmen dorm on my way to class. The Chancellor was building the new dorm to bring a more diverse atmosphere to the school.

The intention of the new dorm was to box the freshmen in their own little community. Encouraging them to eat, play, and study where they lived. The idea of the small learning communities, diversity, a "new way of learning", is what the psychologists were calling this movement.

So, I posed the question. How can one become diverse, meet new people, explore new things if they are sheltered in these small communities? Where is the diversity if you are around the same people all day, everyday? Where is the exploration? Where is the competition? Or better yet, how can you find yourself?

Instead of growing and becoming individuals, I saw that many were conforming to the ways of institution and its many subcultures. In the early studies of psychosocial development, Erikson described this as identity versus role confusion.

Live a little, get out, go somewhere you haven't been. That is why I had to have my car at school with me. I was not going to be stuck on this campus. I was gone somewhere every night.

I've never understood why students try so hard to be a part of the "in crowd". They think that being cool is easy. Many just don't understand that it takes a lot of personal sacrifice to be part of this so-called "in crowd".

I remember back in high school, my homeboy working hard to make it seem as if there was nothing wrong in his life. He was the new kid, but I knew how to play the new kid role also, so that didn't work with me. He would wear the same outfit every three days, but claim he was rich. Rich people don't do that to their children.

It was almost like he was trying to create a character for himself not understanding that it's not your financial status that makes you cool. Not lying makes you cool. I call that sheltered. He was from the country and didn't know that you can't lie to a city boy.

He was performing for an imaginary audience in which he was the main actor. He was in his own world. He made himself into his own personal fable.

One's mind, opinions, and beliefs are all things that one will lose in order to go along with the ideals in which the proverbial "coolest guy" or "coolest group" has control over. I should know. I'm that guy.

I slowed down my jog. "Whaz's happenin" I said to a girl I never saw before.

"Hey," she said knowing what time it was by the look on my face.

"So, in order for us to get to know each other better . . . are you coming to see me or do I have to come see you?" I wasn't going to waste any time with this one. She was ready.

"Your funny, I like that" she replied. She was fine but I could tell she wasn't an athletic type by the little pouch she was forming. One too many keg stands at the Frat house. I figure I would catch her before it got out of control and her belly started looking like a tire which she rested on when tired from breathing. I was going to have to act fast on this one.

"You're cute and I like that," I added to give her that extra security blanket she was asking for when she stopped to talk. "Here, there's no time like the present, so take this and call me as soon as you get out of class," I said as I gave her a piece of paper with my number on it. I was in a public place and her number couldn't go straight into the phone.

"And what are we going to do . . . where are we going?" She wanted to know.

"One step at a time baby, let's get to the point of you calling, then move forward slowly. If we start off too fast then we are going to finish fast. And you don't want that, do you?"

"I guess not." She was so innocent and freaky.

"Use it, don't abuse it."

"Ok," she said as she walked away looking over her shoulder.

Final Thoughts: "If you have the opportunity to be great? Why wait? . . . . . Everyday you have the opportunity to be great! What are you waiting on? . . . . .If you're not moving, you're not making moves . . . . . . don't take anything with you, cause where you are going requires nothing but loyalty."

Chapter II

EDUCATION

"Words can be written, translated, and defined. But can never be taken back once said."

That Same Look

IT was almost 10:15 a.m. when I reached class. The professor gave me that same look she would always give me, as if she really was going to fail me. I grabbed a seat in the back of the classroom and threw my bag on the seat in front of me.

I saw school in one way: as a means to getting what I needed out of life. I knew that I wasn't going to be able to live life without a big house and nice car. In order to have those, I had to have an education.

My trick to the school thing was simple. Statistics show that more than half of the people diagnosed with Alzheimer's disease have a high level of educational background. I wasn't about to fill my head up with all of that Jeopardy knowledge that I was never going to use, causing my brain to give up on me one day. I understood the basic concepts of each subject that I didn't like but needed. In most cases, I was taking them in order to graduate.

In these classes, I would do all the homework and activites good enough to get an A or B. They were usually a worksheet anyways. Who can't do a worksheet? The work was never hard to me. It was just the fact I had to sit there and listen to this teacher teach something that I could had easily had read in a book sitting on my couch. Then, I would interactively, I will repeat, INTERACTIVELY participate in the classes which I would choose to prolong a career.

This was a Biology class, and I could care less about paying attention. I wasn't attending any medical school in the near future. I tried to stay up by playing with people from across the class but then that got old and I started writing down some raps to keep me occupied.

I pulled up, hoped out, da Whip looking clean. Females with big butts only look good in jeans (yeah). Cause they can't do it good, if you know what I mean (really). You can only reign in a realm for SO long. This is a Republic. That's why no King lives ON.
So, I'm going back to the original plan and SAY forget it. Linen and tank tops, flip flops with no socks. Murdering each other on the beach where there're no cops (I Know). It only takes one to die, only takes one to lie, and a couple of homeboys pointing in the sky. For us to understand why.
Don't every think I'll jump the broom. They got Nice houses with no wall. Big houses with no room. And for a mill, a midget can touch the moon. It's like she cute, No brain. Dress nice, but insane. And she wonder why she will never be my main.
I'm giving indicators, You see me touching the hat. So fall back, straight out like a bat. Her juice level real high, I can see it in her eyes. Invested in towing, got the bunnies moving snow.

Ok, that was aight, but I ain't no rapper. Looks more like a Haiku or something. I just had to do something before I went crazy. I never stayed in class, in high school, so I wasn't use to sitting for a long time. It wasn't like I had a disorder. I just didn't want to sit in a class all day. I could have if I wanted but why? I wasn't in the habit of sitting in a class.

Everyone had their notebooks out with their pens in the corner of their mouths as if that was the proper way of sitting in a college class. I was slumped down in my seat with my hat all the way down over my eyes. I could care less.

There were only two black females in my class. There was Kim, who loved me and Sheri, who hated the fact that she couldn't love me. See, my situation is very strange and weird, but makes a lot of sense when you consider the elements. If life was an experiment, my control group would be football and school. Now the experimental group would consist of different males (which are the haters) and females. Trying numerous combinations to establish a hypothesis, execute tests, and develop solid conclusions.

Whenever you include boys and girls, males and females, *Go Get Hers* and *Go Get Hims* in the same place there is sure to be tension. They can just be friends, and there is still going to be sexual tension.

In all, there were a lot of girls that went to my high school and even a lot more women that attend the university. The only real difference is the amount of freedom that a college student has. What exactly do they expect college students to do in our spare time? Study? No. We use our free time to sleep, gain weight, and have relations – as my grandmother would say.

Class was so boring that I had to leave. It was nice outside, and since I was sitting by the window I could see how much fun everyone was having that wasn't in class. I leaned over and put my arm around Kim's chair.

"I'm out," I whispered to Kim. She helps me do my work. She's cool with it and only expects me to come to class for a little while to show that I at least care a little.

"You don't need to leave . . . you know we are having a test next week," she whispered fiercely.

"You got me, don't you?" I gave her one of my puppy dog looks and started a little moan to solidify the deal.

"Go ahead, but you have to come and get these notes."

"You cooking?" I replied.

"Yeah," she said quickly.

"I'll be there," I stated as I eased out my seat and exited out the back.

Walking through campus was a carnival. People were protesting, others were politicking, and most were in a rush to go absolutely nowhere. People were just everywhere on campus. It was a typical Wednesday, I guess.

I really didn't have anywhere to go, so I strolled around campus. I went to my mailbox, talked with the ladies in the café, and hollered at a couple of people I already knew. I felt like taking the whole day off, but I had to go to weight training in an hour.

That was enough time to go to the room and grab my bag. The late summer air brought about a time of couple-making. People looking to lock up with someone before the winter came. The atmosphere was intense. With each day another game was in session.

There was a mixture of different people and different situations that I observed scrolling through campus. Most classes were over and the oh-so-valuable leisure time for a college student, was present. Everyone was looking for conformity, knowing where they were to fit in. Many were trying to find the right blend of people to grow to one's fullest potential.

With me, three factors come with every situation. The first factor is me, the main ingredient. I could become whatever I wanted to: a lawyer, teacher, promoter, or a bum, it didn't matter. It was up to me.

The second factor is a role player. The role player is key, usually a homeboy, a loyal person that will help guide you through certain situations. A role player is very essential to survival.

The last factor is the X-factor. The X-factor is called a hater. This would be the variable or the unknown of the experiment.

Most people don't realize haters because they don't realize human nature.

Two females were looking like they were going to approach me as I was leaving out the front of the dorm room. I would have said something to them but the timing wasn't right. I wanted to catch them on a one on one basis. I could tell that both of them were attracted to me. Ain't no fun if her home girl can't have none.

The same reason that females were attracted to me was the same reason that haters were. The rules of attraction established by Eagly in 1991 states that physical attraction is the first linking. The second was proximity, being close. The third was similarity; taking on similar characteristics. Then last was when the opposite is attracted; haters getting close.

People were attracted to pride, fame, and money; the root of all evil. I have money, I have fame, and I have more pride than a picky beggar, which in my eyes means that I had the power.

I got over to the complex twenty minutes before I had to be there. It gave me a chance to do something I been meaning to do for the longest. Get a good stretch. I had been complaining about my legs but never could find time to get a good stretch with my schedule being the way that it was.

Time Management

I ran into the locker room because I had to use the bathroom. I could hear my phone going off from inside the bathroom stall. I shook twice and jogged over to check my phone before it was my turn on the bench press again. I had three missed calls. It wasn't anybody important enough to call back. I threw the phone back on my sweat pants and went back in the weight room.

Mirrors covered every inch of the weight room walls. My body was right. Half of my teammates were already starting to take off layers of clothing trying to show the hard work they were putting into their workout. I wasn't about to show off for no males, doing all that yelling and screaming to get the team pumped. I was a pure athlete, I didn't need any motivation. I performed when called upon.

I got back under the bench and started lifting as if I had a fat girl on top of me. "Get that big girl off of you!" I heard someone say as I pushed up what weighed almost three hundred pounds. I finished my workout with a few more reps on the curl bar to make sure that everything was tight. I didn't mind working out. Having to deal with all the other things that came during the course of the day was the problem. Dealing with things like trying to find something to eat and dealing with fake people was worst than lifting.

As we wrapped everything up, most of the guys were still lingering in the locker room. Females were always the topic of conversation. I could tell that some freshmen football players were having a terrible time out of their comfort zone. I could tell by the way they were talking that they truly didn't understand what was going on.

I guess that's why I never felt I had to ever step up my game around them. My student body was mostly a mixture of country boys thrown into a little city environment. They hadn't been around many women and didn't know how to act. Actions speak a lot louder than words until you say something stupid. I had my crew and the football team, other than them, it was females. I couldn't have random dumb people around me.

I jumped in the shower and washed the triangle, under both arms and the mid section. The big boys were in the shower throwing soap so I had to put on my "not today" face.

Playing in the shower was something I just didn't do. My locker was about like my room . . . junky. I looked at my locker and just started throwing away all the paper that was taking over my seat: phone numbers, football plays, past due school assignments. Everything was just thrown in different folders.

Baggage can mean a lot of different things, not just suitcases and carry-on bags. How much you talk on the phone or how much time you spend doing any particular thing takes away from other important things you can be doing. You can never become obsessed with one particular task. It will drive you crazy.

Time management was a class that every freshman had to take. I missed the first two sessions. When I attended the last one the most important information that I got out of it was to cut off ignorant people and unnecessary activities out of your schedule.

After throwing all my papers in the trash, I saw the opportunity to dip out without anyone saying anything to me. I was tired and needed a couple of hours of sleep before I hit the streets again. One thing that I have learned is that people who have not seen the struggle do not understand the power and energy it takes to progress through the situation. And I was struggling to stay up. I was finding out very quickly that sleep was an un-fightable battle.

Life was hard, but college is the one place where I could still be young. I had to get all the partying out of my system before getting married and starting on my successful career. I stood up.

My bag was kind of heavy as I tossed it over my shoulder. As I bent over to pick up the last piece of paper, sweat raced to the floor in front of me. I sat back down and gathered myself before leaving.

I must have sat there for two minutes wiping my face from the profuse puddles coming from my forehead. My body was hot like a middle-aged women going through menopause. The air must have been off, once again I was up and now walking out the locker room.

As I hit the door, I ran into one of the ex-football players. He graduated about six years ago but still comes around. He was lame so I just gave him a head nod at first.

One of my deepest fears was that I would be that old guy still trying to hang out on a college campus. A mid-life crisis was definitely at the bottom of the list.

"You aight," I said sliding past him, and in the process letting him know I was on the scene now.

I just couldn't stand those old college guys. Everyone knows that one thirty year old that still goes to the campus parties. I was not going to be that guy.

I didn't look back as I went through the door. I just smiled and kept my charisma. I imagined my picture being up in the Athletic Hall of Fame as I walked through the corridors. Great warriors were all along the walls, and history was displayed. Faces of victory and triumph rang out from the black and white photos.

I was going to leave my mark just as those who had come before me. As I hit the door, it became party time again. Ladies were jogging, reading, and sunbathing: everything that motivated me. This was the first time that a thousand of females are out of their parent's homes and willing to party till they drop. The use of experimental drugs was as common as two fat girls at a buffet. My story was a little different in certain ways because of who I was, but I still was like every other freshman that had eyes.

I went to every party and tried to get with every female that was looking for an after party. It was obvious who they were, and it was easy to approach them by asking, "Do you want a drink?" If they said that they did not drink, that was the clue to push the issue that everyone else was doing it. If a male can get a female to buy into drinking then it usually ends up being one of the best nights he will ever have in his life. If she did drink, than it was Go Time.

I went back to my room and laid down. I needed a drink by now. As I began to look around the room, the pictures began to remind me of the good old times in high school, hanging out and just kicking it until six in the morning. The parties here were nothing compared to back home. That's probably why I started to drink. In order to really enjoy myself, I had to be drunk.

Then I thought about joining a social group to keep me busy, but that came to pass during the first couple of days. Everyone wanted me to join their own particular organization. I just felt like if I joined one group then how would the others feel? I didn't want to upset anyone so I decided to get along with everyone. Plus, I remembered what Poppa said about submitting.

The door to my room was wide open. Someone was playing music down the hallway. There weren't any lights on in my room except the light coming from the TV. I flicked through all the channels before turning back and watching the same episode of Sports Center that I saw earlier in the locker room. My bladder was full from drinking three protein shakes, and my stomach was starting to turn. I got up and went to the bathroom.

It looked like everyone was just about to go out for dinner. People were hanging outside each others doors asking the same question. "So where are we eating?"

I knew because I got that question about five times a night. I was the "in-crowd". I was the leader you could say. Don't believe me, watch this.

"Hey man, come here," I asked this random guy walking down the hall.

"What's up?"

"Where da ladies at?" I asked.

"Aw man, you got all da ladies"

See I told ya.

I was known for many things, but mostly known for having many females. Every decision that I made was for the good or bad of everyone around me. I felt my actions gave everyone around me confidence to say what they wanted to say and act how they wanted to act. This was my fault. I knew what I was doing and DIDN'T care.

I was the captain of my ship, I was in control. Most of my life was like that, and it took my senior year in high school to realize that people were using me to get what they wanted. School became a cat and mouse culture. It was a race to the cheese. It became a game to see who could make it.

Everything was a game. We had football games, basketball games, and relationship games. The only difference in the relationship game is that people tend to forget that it is a game, and should never involve emotions or someone will get hurt. People forget that love is an emotion just like anger, and just as anger, love will cause you to commit an irrational act.

Baby Girl

The freshmen experience is one big circus, "testing the waters" as we say. The first time you take a drink, or the first time that you take a hit, these are all games that we play whether by ourselves or with other people. What people don't realize is that in order to play any game you have to know the rules.

Have you ever been around a Monopoly game? When everyone knows the rules it's organized and business is handled. If one doesn't know the rules, the other players will make sure that he is out quick. They gain control of the game that way. One has to realize that when a person doesn't know the information they need to suceed in a game, other members can talk over your head because you don't know what is going on anyways. Knowledge of the game is key.

My phone rang. "Hey baby." It was Amber.

"What's up?"

"Are we still going to the movies, cause we can go to the off-campus movie theater. I just need to know so I can get the tickets."

"That's cool. I don't get out of practice until seven, so what time are you trying to go?" I replied

"Just call me when you get out of practice, and I will let you know," Amber said.

"No, let me know now so you can't blame me for being late. I'm going to be on time." I had to make it clear just in case we didn't make it on time, it wouldn't be my fault.

"7:45," she said sounding not really sure but just to make it a date.

Like most guys in college, I have a main girl, Amber. She was everything that completed me, my soul-mate, for the time being. Amber was elegant and very intellectual. She had smooth fair skin that looked liked caramel, and juicy red lips that tasted like strawberries with a little hint of love.

Amber was the total package; fine, rich, with not that much common sense. Amber was what every man wanted, a lady in the streets and someone that gets loose in the sheets. Right? Amber was the baddest one on campus, and I had her.

Amber and I met right before we came to college. We were at a senior cut party, and she walked by me. I stuck my leg out and tripped her with my foot accidently. Ok, I did it on purpose. After we had words about the whole tripping matter and figured out who was who, then everything was cool.

See, I was *the man* at my high school. She had heard about me through other people. I heard she really didn't like talking to boys that went to my school. She felt we were all bred the same: *cruel and heartless*. All that changed when she met me.

I came at her with a different approach than any other guy she had ever been with. I first greeted her with a "Hi". Instead of treating her like hunting bait, I listened and asked her questions that interested her. I swept her off her feet. We kept finding out different things that intrigued both of us, which led to us uncovering the news that we were going to be attending the same university.

All of this happened the day before I left for school. She came to see me every weekend for the two months in the summer before camp started. Since I was already settled in when she got there, I helped her move into her dorm. I've been over there ever since.

Our relationship was good and with no drama up to this point. We were the model couple on campus. The upper-class guys where hating on me because they wanted her, and the upper-class girls where hating on her because they wanted me. It was a beautiful situation.

Amber was also the one that I introduced to my mom when I came to the house to pick up some more of my things. Not too many girls can meet Mom in that short frame of time. She was bad. If your mom likes your girl, she is a keeper (for the time being). I kept all of the other girls in my life around in order to satisfy my self-esteem and my desire for power.

Males thirst for power within a female and male relationships in order to feel superior. This is the real reason why men don't want their wives making more money in the household. It's due to the fact that most times the person that makes the most money is in control: providing for the wants and not the needs of the family is power.

I was nothing like that. I wanted my female to be rich, forget that. It's nothing more unattractive than a broke female. Broke females shouldn't be allowed to leave the house.

I sat down in the stall once I got back to the room, and there was a newspaper article that I picked up. It read 'Relationships: The Endless Battle." I am a firm believer that you can't win a battle if you don't know who you are fighting. See, I was fighting Asmodeus, the demon of Lust. This was the same demon that messed with King Solomon and Samson. Now he was after me. I was a fighter and not worried about any demon of lust. I have ties with Diablo. Asmodeus had to answer to him. I had Amber, but the temptation of female companionship was brawny.

Over the course of my short life, I have been called a lot of names by different females: dog, pimp, player, buster, and even a female dog. It even went as far that I was delivered dog biscuits every morning.

I prefer to be called a "teacher" or "coach." Everyone knows the saying "you should learn something new, every day". Well, I try to teach something new every day. I feel that life is a big lesson. One's actions are based on his knowledge and experiences. If you want to know about a person, see how they act in front of their grandparents.

I didn't have any plans for after practice so this was a good weekday to go to the movies. I needed to relax anyways. Amber and I had only been talking for three months now (since May). I enjoyed being with her.

Taking her places like the movies and out to eat was straight with me because those were things I like to do anyways. I was still comfortable about our relationship. I mean my past was not pleasant, and I knew my future wasn't promised. I was a man of the land and lived everyday like there was no tomorrow.

Mentally, I was born into the royal family. I was always told to walk around with my head up high. In my earlier life, all the aspects of becoming a great man were taught to me daily. My need for women was always present and their presence was always welcome: sneaking around, not having parents breathing down your back, my own room, not having any limitations. If you're not having fun in college, you don't know what you are missing.

Final Thoughts: "If you listen to your teacher and be obedient in their ways, then no harm will come to you. For one day you will become the teacher and their ways will become yours."

Chapter III

THE GREATEST STRUCTURE

"In order to be great, you have to be around great things. In order to get money, you have to be around people with money. In order to be a KING, one must understand LOYALTY, ROYALTY, and HONOR."

The Foundation

It seemed as if everyone was getting into their normal routine. I had found out the exact route to take in order to run into all the cute girls. My campus was beautiful. There was a lake about two miles from campus that brought on the feeling as if we were close to a beach. The tension in the air was that much stronger. The energy was growing as everyone was getting geared up to play the first home game of the season this weekend.

I stopped at the water faucet in the hallway of the dorm. I had to meet Amber in ten minutes. My outfit was already lying out. I only had my light on in the room because I had to hurry up and find another clean sock. I should have had one of these girls do my laundry yesterday.

They were mix matched, but it was cool because they were both low cut. I could just tuck them in so it would look like I didn't have on any socks at all. I threw on some Him cologne first. Then I threw on my Du Rag. Brushing my hair with the Du Rag on was how my waves would pop out. I was never the disappointment when I was out with a lady.

I was in the car within the next five minutes. I sent her a text message to say I was on the way. Her dorm was across the way so she knew that meant to come on out. I'm glad I cleaned the truck. I had all kind of loose articles in the back seat. She was sure to look back and find something when I was driving. So I just eliminated that whole headache before it started.

It was a good night to go out. There weren't that many people moving around. It was 7:20 so we had a little time to get to the movies before I missed the previews. I was trying to convince her to see another movie, but she had her heart set on this one particular movie. I had seen it with another girl, but I couldn't tell her that. I hated having to see the same movie three times in the same week. About mid-way between the second go round I was usually sleep.

"Hey baby," Amber said as she jumped in the truck, then leaned over and gave me a kiss.

"How was your day?" I replied as I pulled off and made a right out of the complex.

Amber was stunning. She had her hair pulled back with a cute little outfit on. "I see ya" I said acknowledging the fact that she caught my eye.

"Too bad you can't upgrade from me. I'm on top," I said as she grabbed my hand. My palm was open and resting on the middle console.

See, every male's mind allows them to see the game as a pyramid, the greatest structure built by the Egyptians during 2630-2611 BC. The Pyramid Age started with Pharaoh Zoser who left his identification in the underground chambers of the great monuments that he had built for himself.

So, during my research of great civilization and kings, I have found that every male keeps private records out of the public eye. Every male dating back to these ancient times also has his own version of a black book.

I turned my phone on silent because it keep ringing. It rang twice on the ride there so I put it in my pocket as we walked in and just said forget it. If someone needed me they were going to have to wait until the end of the movie.

Only four people were already in their seats. The dim lights were still on and the big screen was showing concession stands commercials. We were still early so I went back out into the lobby to get some candy and drinks. Those ads got to me.

"Where do I know this 319 number from?" I asked myself. "Oh ah, this was that little cute girl Casey I had met by the bar yesterday." So, I decided to call her up to see what she was doing. I had about two minutes to get a solid conversation out that included time, dates, and plans. I knew what I was getting myself into even before I approached her at the bar last night. I do my research on every female that I approach to reduce all possibility of getting turned down.

At the club that night, I had played it real cool and took a spot near where she was standing. I got in perfect position to make the first eye contact. Females like Casey can see potential in any male. Just be real. It will make everyone's college experience a lot better. I'm not saying she was a gold digger. What I am saying is she is an educated female who strategically plans out how to attract a rich man. There is nothing wrong with that. Make that money.

I sat back and watched Casey from across the room. She had already turned down three guys. The way she was looking and her demeanor let me know what she was all about. She didn't want no lame. She was waiting for a guy like me to come show her a good time.

See, Casey was a "crab." I already knew this. Me and my boys call girls crabs when they claim to have not had any relations with anybody. The word 'crab' comes from when a girl has already had relations but is trying to hold on to her 'v card'. Many times they say things like, "I don't have relations, I don't drink, and I don't smoke." Yeah whatever, pee on me and call it rain.

I really wish that they would put that aspect on the application when trying to attend a college or university. GPA should stand for "Girls Practicing Abstinence." Casey was a prime example of a crab trying to hold on to her 'v card'.

I even knew some of the other guys she messed with. My older brother told me one time that, "Virgins were like homeless people. Once you treat them nice, they start making themselves at home. And no one wants to take in a homeless person."

The line at the concession was short so I stood back and looked at the menu acting as if I was going to buy one of those expensive combo meals. The phone started ringing.

For males, when making the first phone call you must start off by playing the role as if we have forgotten the number and are trying to remember who she is. She had already called my phone so she just made my job that much easier. I would make the call back and then say that she caught me at a bad time, ending the conversation quickly. This method always should work, unless the female has absolutely no clue of who you are during the callback. Then just hang up and go to the next number because it's a lost cause anyways.

Everybody has a club name because that is how you keep your name out of the streets. I went by Lo most of the time. I would play games based on what type of girl I was talking with. If a hood rat asked why my name was Lo, I would look at her real dirty and tell her to use her imagination. She would often grin and then we would move on into a nice conversation.

If it was a classy girl I would tell her that my name was Lew, along with some sad story that would blow her mind: maybe something like I grew up around white people, and then add in a good old fashioned poor story to make things interesting. Depends on what type of female I am dealing with.

In learning how to relate to people, the icebreaker is important. It usually expains a person's personality and attitude. If someone is shy, words do not have to be present when meeting someone new. Non-verbal communication should present some type of energy or personal connection. So when I called back it sounded like this.

"Hello," she said. It sounded like she either was listening to the radio or watching television.

"Whaz happenin. Did someone call this number?" I replied in a deep, but not to deep, voice. I knew who it was, but I couldn't just come out and say it.

"I was looking for Lo."

"Who is this?" I had to keep playing the high road to gain control over the conversation.

"Casey" she then replied. There was a weird little pause in our conversation because we were both trying to ask each other something at the same time.

"Do you know who I am?" she went on to add. "We met at NV Tuesday?" she said before I could say anything.

"Yeah," I said calm and under control.

"Were you by the bar?" Now she asks the question.

"Yeah. OK. I think I know who this might be. What did you have on?"

"I had on a green dress."

Ok. Now let's evaluate the conversation thus far. First, during a phone conversation, males should always have a list of questions in their head in order to keep the conversation going. Secondly, if she can recognize your voice and pen-point where she knows you from she is trouble. And thirdly, I say this for every female. If you answer the question "What did you have on?" you're stupid. If a male meets a female for the first time and can't remember what she had on, he don't like you. Ya'll only exchanged numbers to have relations (as my grandmother would say).

I got off the phone with Casey as I grabbed my candy and drink from the concession. I was about to make a big mistake and drink straight from the cup but I used the straw instead. I didn't want to ruin my new shirt. I might have to wear it again soon. I even went to the mall and picked up two outfits this past weekend. One was a blue velour Prada outfit and the other was a yellow Gucci sweat suit to wear with my gold teeth. Yeah, I got some gold teeth.

I had eight gold teeth at the bottom to be exact. They are pull outs, and I only wear them to the club. I know that thugs don't go to college and everything else that goes along with having a respectable image. I heard it all from my mom. Well I got them so live with it. I'm sorry I got a little emotional. Where was I?

One thing about going out to clubs is that no matter how fresh or sharp you feel you are, there is always going to be someone dressed a little better than you. We call it "paining". When you left the house feeling like a billion bucks, you thought you were fresh. Then comes the pain. It hurts on the inside and leaves a certain burning pain when you see that another person took your shine. Whether it is the dub on your car, the beat in your ride, a cell phone with ring tones, screens in the Lac, DVD's in the back or a fat wad of money so you and your boys can floss with a couple stacks: you will be pained.

So, when picking out an outfit I suggest clearance stores for the college student of tomorrow. Burlington or TJ Maxx is my Mecca for urban wear. You can buy a whole outfit for the nifty fifty (50 dollars). Why spend money when you don't have to? This also leaves money for flossing. Twenty dollars here and there can really come in handy in the long run, especially for a college student.

The lights were already off as I entered the movie theater. The first preview was just coming on. Amber was seated with her legs crossed but threw one of them on top of mine as I sat next to her. I checked my phone one more time before putting it back in my pocket. I put it on silent because I knew she would be able to feel if it vibrating. I wrapped my arm around her and got comfortable. This night was over with for everyone else. I was with Amber for the time, and she was going to get all of my attention.

The Pyramid

We both found ourselves falling asleep at the movie. Once again, that movie was not worth the money I paid to go see it. First, the old guy didn't want to die. Then the children were too stupid to realize what the next door neighbor was trying to tell them. Well, we left and went back to Amber's room.

The air was on in Amber's room so I took some of her socks to sleep in. By the time I woke up, I was barefoot and freezing. I liked sleeping over there; it was just the fact that she had a community bathroom that I didn't like. I would wake up with 'morning pee' and couldn't just step into my personal lavatory.

The floor didn't have any carpet so I had to hurry and put on my shoes. My football shorts had pockets. I slid my phone into the little one that was on the waist line. My phone is my personal assistant. It keeps phone numbers, important dates, current time, emails, text messages, and everything else that I didn't know how to work. It was my own private black book.

A black book is a basic tablet in which a male keeps private records. In ancient times they wrote on the walls of caves, then papyrus, then paper, and now with the modern day cell phone. Every situation has to have rules and guidelines as we know. Certain persons can't interact with certain other people. Certain rules must be followed in order to keep playing the game fair.

I stood in the mirror as I washed the morning sand out of my eyes. Today was going to be long, and my stomach was already starting to hurt. It was 7:15 a.m. and everyone was still sleep. The janitors always cleaned the girls' bathroom a little better than the boys. That's why I liked sneaking in the female bathroom instead of the males.

I heard someone about to come in so I took a stall and laid low for a minute. It was a white girl about to get in the shower, so I went on and took my morning boo boo since I was just sitting there. I began to check my messages from the night before.

"You have seven new messages," my female personal assistant told me as I dialed the voicemail. I had to courtesy flush a couple of times or else she would have known it was a male and not a female. I would throw-up if a female smelled like this. The first couple of messages were from my grandma telling me the same thing in bits and pieces. She didn't know how to use her cell phone quite yet. The others were from credit card companies and young ladies.

I got up and slid out of the door without scaring the little white girl. I had my shirt off. My tattoo game was just getting started. I believed that my body was a temple. I dressed my temple accordingly with markings of significant value. My theories and ideas of life stood out in bold tribal symbols.

My life was a structured monument: a Pyramid. One of the greatest structures ever built, the pyramid is a solid structure with deceptively remarkable attributes. Built on the bases of cornerstones and a strong frame is what gives the pyramid the ability to withstand time.

The top of the pyramid is where my Three-Point Star Theory takes place. The Three-Point Star, an unbreakable triangle which consists of three characteristic traits of mastering the game based on superior knowledge. Royalty, loyalty, and respect are what make the three sides bond.

Royalty is my idea that a man is in a consistent search for his Queen. The top of the pyramid contains three females. The Princess sits at the top with her two attendants. These two attendants consist of the next two candidates in line to become a

Princess, if something happens. One should always have a royal court. No one is perfect, so the idea of having a court is to satisfy one's appetite.

Loyalty is the mental state that comes with the sharing of ideas and dream with the person you feel is capable of being your Queen. Relationships are based upon how deeply involved you are with a person, but this is the trick. Everyone can have a relationship with everyone you come in contact with, but how deep the relationship goes determines how long it will last.

And the last aspect is Respect. This comes in the fact that most women know that their man is cheating. With the Princess, the Prince must show respect in order to keep happiness in the kingdom and uphold the laws of courtship. The respect level for the Prince and Princess are both extremely high. We might debate and have disagreements but we will never disrespect each other in public or in private.

I didn't want to wake Amber because I knew she didn't have class until eleven o'clock. I sat at the edge of the bed and used the light coming from under the door to put the rest of my clothes on.

I sat there for a minute and just watched her sleep. She was peaceful. I kissed her on the forehead as I grabbed my overnight bag and went out the door. Only one female can be at the top of your pyramid. Amber was at the top of mine. There must be order in this grand scheme. I never tried to have more than one main girl. Poor preparation will leave you out in the cold.

The reality is that the Princess, Amber, knows what I'm doing. But I respect her and didn't let any disrespectful actions come her way. Her life should be stress free. As Prince, I should make sure that no drama reaches the potential first lady's ears. I say I never cheat because lust and love are two different things. While lust comes over a male's mind countless times throughout the day, my genuine selfless love represent the highest degree of development in our relationship.

Amber was the only girl that I would stop anything and everything for, no matter what. Amber was the acting Princess of my temple, which I was building for my family. So I treated the top of my pyramid like royalty, and Amber was treated as if she was just that, a Princess.

Love gives the inkling of loyalty with another person in a relationship. Lust can only be described as the excessive desire for releasing sexual tension. The other person can therefore be seen as a "means to an end" for the fulfillment of the subject's desires, and thus becomes objectified in the process. In an ancient story about a guy named Purgatorio, he would walk through flames to purge himself of lustful thoughts. It wasn't that serious to me.

My car was already warm because I used my automatic crank from inside the building. I turned the music up to get my morning started off right. I was thinking about even getting some breakfast and going to class. Instead I called someone to see what they were cooking.

"You up?" Brooke was a senior that stayed in the off-campus apartments. She was a morning person so I knew she had to be up.

"I'm up."

"Well then open the door," I commanded even though I wasn't there yet.

"It's open. Where are you?" She was a little dingy, but it was cool.

"I'm parking now."

Brooke has been a long member of the middle of my pyramid. The middle of my pyramid consists of ex-girlfriends, your friends that are a little more than just a friend, on-going relations partners, and girls that know about your girlfriend but don't care. Brooke was considered a friend that was a little more than a friend.

This is the meat of the structure. The most fruitful part in which, being part of a royal family, one takes heed to in order to sow his royal oats. I consider this section of my temple "the holding cell".

In any diagram of a pyramid, there were always "holding cells" that were located around the middle area of the structure. This area was usually found on the opposite end in which you would find the Queen's sleeping quarters, which was not surprising.

Brooke was cool and could cook a breakfast that would put you right back in the bed. I sat on the couch as she brought me plate after plate of sausages, eggs, and pancakes. She was older and was looking for a serious relationship to get into. That's not going to happen.

The second level is the group that I had to keep my eye on because some of them might experience emotional attachment. This category has the most potential of causing turnover. Each member of the mid-section wants their chance at the top. They don't quite have what it takes to become number one but the effort is tremendous. If they ever feel that they need a little more attention, then actions will need to be taken to secure the entire structure. Corruption cannot be tolerated therefore action must take place.

I didn't want too stay to long. I wanted to make it very clear what I was over there for. Breakfast. It was almost nine o'clock by now, and I had to go over to the athletic complex to get a little treatment on my ankle. By going to treatment, I didn't have to do anything in practice. It was a sweet situation since I was already in the neighborhood.

I walked in the training room a little after nine. Our training room was state-of-the-art: swimming pools, aerobic equipment, the whole nine.

I had to include all my haters in the mid-section, due to the fact that you always have to keep your eyes on a hater more than your friends. My head trainer was a hater. He saw how I talked to every female that was in the training room. He didn't like it but couldn't help it.

He would often do little childish things like make me move all the way to the other side of the room if he thought I was talking to someone that was in there getting treatment. He would try to treat me like I was a kid in time out. He was a lame.

The key to protecting the mid-area is taking the attachment element out of the equation. Attachment is the element that converts a relationship from the physical to the mental side.

A prime example of something not to do is sleep in the same bed as a female where there isn't any sexual activities taking place. I found that in situations like that, if the female feels that she can just lay up with a male then she feels that having *baby making* practices shouldn't be an issue. The practice of *baby making* is always an issue when dealing with relationships. Feeling that strong sexual attraction is what keeps the love alive. Once that connection is lost so is the love, and it then becomes a mere commitment arrangement were one feels obligated.

Most males often get caught-up in the relationship question. Due to the fact that females often want to know, "Where do I fit in your life?" "Where are we in our relationship?" The answer is always the same with me. Like before, I believe that I have a relationship with every female that I come in contact with. Now, it's on them how fast, deep, and memorable our relationship can grow.

"Back in here again?" the defensive line coach said as he walked by me with a smirk on his face. "Wont ever get on the field staying in here," he concluded, walking so fast I didn't have a chance to say something smart back to him. I didn't like that. I wanted to be red-shirted now. Give me a year to get right. A lot of our coaches acted like that for some reason, like that was supposed to encourage me.

I had my eyes on this track girl that was lying face down on the table. She knew what she was doing. Her backside was all in the air. She was wearing some shorts that looked like panties from a distance. Females become so obvious about what type of relationship they are looking for based on how they dress.

I never bought into the notion that it is ok to dress like a prostitute. Prostitutes dress like prostitutes, and ladies dress like ladies. I can play around with the middle of the structure because the base is what keeps me going.

Her face wasn't that cute, but her booty was so properly proportioned I couldn't help but to want to have relations. Based on appearance alone, she was going to fit well within the bottom of the pyramid. Her face wasn't up to par so that meant no public interaction, just face meetings. Face meetings are meetings that are face to face somewhere private.

Now the base or foundation of my structure was strong. The respect level is very high for the base of my pyramid. I love the base of my pyramid for three reasons. They listen even if they don't understand, they participate even when they don't want to, and they know their role and play the game like a pro. I love these extraordinary females.

The base consisted of females that know me for one purpose and one purpose only. Party-animal. These selected females knew that at any given time they can call me for a great night. Our phone conversations are always short, and I always leave these girls feeling like I forgot to pay them for their service. No disrespect.

There was one occasion when I almost gave a girl my next months rent, but we are not going to talk about that. The respect level is tremendous for my bottom females. I only respect them because they understand and respect the game. I have so much respect for them that I started calling them "well-qualified females", due to the fact that if I needed something done, I would call the most qualified female at the time.

In looking at why males love bottom females, you would have to learn about different spiritual demons. The Succubus is the demon of lust that sleeps with men in order to impregnate their minds so that they can manifest lust. The Incubi demon sleeps with women to lead them astray and to impregnate them with demon manifestation. That's why everyone is consistently thinking about lustful acts.

I sat there in the training room and watched how the track girl rolled over and moved her body. She wanted me to notice her. She turned towards me and put both of her knees in her chest. I just sat there and watched. Everything that she was doing was geared towards me approaching her later.

My entire basis of how females act comes solely from observing. Within my observation of females, I found that they too have a pyramid. The whole female concept is different and unknown to most men. Their pyramid relates to the evolution of the female mind. Their understanding of how men act is on their experiences through life. Weather the female is naive or well experienced, is the bases on how she acts within a relationship. How they have been treated by men reflects heavily.

I began understanding the difference between a female that grew up without a 'strong male parent' in the household, and the one's that did. I could tell when a female was lacking a father figure. Certain attachment and discontent for certain activities will start to play within your relationship.

There are three types of females when it comes to building a relationship: a lady, a female dog, and a female cow. A lady is what every man wants. Someone that is sweet, sensitive to his needs, and cares about what he cares about. The other two types of females are basically the same, they're both animals.

The only different between a female dog and a female cow is simply this. A female dog is going to bark all night without letting you play with her. But with a female cow, you can sneak up on her during the middle of the night and tip her over. I can't stand a female dog. I would rather play with a cow in the middle of the night.

I sat there in the training room with the ice on my ankle trying to lay still. I didn't want her to have the upper hand in tormenting me so I stripped down to my under armor, and gave her a good chance to see the bulge in my tights. I was finished by now, so I took the ice off and walked out with all my clothes in my hand. I could see her head turn to my direction as I peaked out of the corner of my eye. She wanted a real man in her life.

There is no logic behind good girls liking bad guys. It's solely has to deal with survival. Females are more comfortable around a male that can support them though physical and mental stability. They want someone that is tough with street smarts.

Attraction also has to deal with the level of energy that a person possesses. In trying to explain how energy effects a person would be tough. Just know that energy is never created or destroyed. That is called Karma. But I will explain how the physical attraction plays a big part.

Every male should be able to notice how females use their looks to separate themselves. Telling and treating an attractive woman like she is average gives the man the upper hand. The same as if we made our women cover up so beauty is never a question when dealing with capability. You have to bring her energy down to your level. Have you ever been around a person that just had too much energy? This is the same type of situation. If you notice some females are like that, too.

Place attractive females all on an even playing field with everyone else, and let's see who has some sense about themselves. I would usually walk right by a female that thought she looked good just to make the point that, "Ain't no one looking at you."

Look at rich people for example. I have nothing against rich people, but most of them are ugly. The power of money and the influence that it has on a person's soul makes them powerful. And power is attractive.

The not so good-looking (let me stop being nice . . . those ugly girls) have no choice in the type of male that comes their way. This forces them to sometimes lose all of their morals and fall into a materialistic society. The pleasure that a cute girl has in making a male pay for something is the same pleasure that an ugly girl gets out of bragging that she had relations with someone. Not being pure should never be something that you broadcast.

I know there is someone for everyone, but some people need to be more humble about being ugly. Be comfortable being you. Forget everyone else. Most people consider themselves to be ten pieces on a ten to one cute scale. I mean, let's be real. If you are an eight then date an eight. Now on the other hand, if you are a three then don't try to date a person that is an eight. Date a three.

Modern Day Black Book

Practice was quick, just the way I liked it. We were finished by seven o'clock, and everyone was in the dining hall getting something to eat. I was tired. I had been up since seven this morning and still hadn't taken my daily nap.

I was usually the last person in the café because I took my sweet time. Nothing was different about today. I sat there with my phone out as I scooped the last piece of pasta in my mouth. My phone is my modern day black book. People just don't write down their numbers anymore, instead they just put them straight into the other person's phone.

In following my idea of the pyramid structure, I had to arrange my phone accordingly. I began to recognize numbers that I had not used in months. As I sat back and thought about my life, my phone conversations dictated most of it.

It's ringing now.

"Hello," I didn't recognize the number, but it looked familiar so I could pick it up.

"I hear you have a girl now," I couldn't distinguish the voice, and I knew it had to be someone that was calling from someone else's phone. Playing.

"Ok," I said calmly. There was a pause in the air. I guess she thought that I was going to deny all allegations. Whoever it was didn't expect the truth.

"Who is this anyways?" I asked.

"La-La," she said as if I was supposed to remember her voice after this long time.

"What's up girl? What are you doing tonight?" I completely disregarding her initial statement.

"You ain't doing anything with your girl?" she asked trying to stay on that subject.

"Not tonight," I replied.

"Oh," she didn't have anything to say. I guess since we had some relations last week she thought she was my girl.

"Stop playing games." I hung up. I would have erased her number, but I had to make sure I didn't answer the next time she called. I saved the number under 'don't answer'. She was playing games. All she wanted was to tell me that I was a dog, but I already knew that. I didn't need anyone to tell me that.

Either she was down with my movement or not. I'm not living anyone else's dream. It's hard enough trying to accomplish mine without someone trying to stop me. That whole conversation was a waste of time and a waste of daytime minutes.

Imagine, during the hours of 9:00 in the morning until 9:00 at night for thirty days, they expect us to use only 500 minutes. You do the math; it's like fifteen minutes a day between those twelve hours. I liked it because that meant that only business was handled during the day. I didn't need unlimited minutes. I never did like someone calling me whenever they felt, just because I had free minutes.

Those phone plans give someone that goes to sleep at ten or eleven o'clock two to three hours to talk. For me, I was up all night so it felt like my phone was unlimited. I hated the day they came out with those Metros and Unlimited everything plans. I can't have my phone ringing all day. How could I get any work done? But there is a reason for everything and I think that I have figured it out.

I put my tray up and said my goodbyes to the café workers. I had to be nice to the people that fed me. The two ladies that worked in the back looked and acted like my aunties. They often called me son and gave me extra food to take back to my room.

"See ya'll," I said as I slid my tray down to the trash dispensor. My phone started to ring again. I wasn't going to answer this time. La-La was trying to call back.

I realized that the CEOs and presidents of these phone companies were not pimps and had no kind of order within their day. Everything was work, work, work. They never understood the concept of setting up your day and putting your priorities in order. They were lame computer kids that always wanted to keep in touch with a cute girl. Call her to tell things you can't in person.

This was my inverted triangle model of communication. The number of people that can be contacted grows larger as the day goes on. This allows a male an ample amount of time to talk to his main girl, and his main girl only, during the day. So don't get mad if some guy or girl does not call you until late. You just fall into that category of nights and weekends.

Text messaging is just another form of leaving a message. Don't feel as if you should get an immediate response. If you wanted the answer right away you would have called. You just left a message. First it was the answering machine, then the beeper, and now text message. I check my text messages when I get home just as if it was an answering machine.

I started calling just random people. I had to think about who I was going to be with because that is very vital to the equation. I needed the right combination of males that knew where to go and females that knew how to get back to where they came from.

Most males pick out a starting line-up of females. They try to set them up like ducks at a circus rifle stand. In order to have the most successful weekend, you have to knock down the most ducks. The more I knocked down, the more successful I became. This was my own law of averages for the mathematically inclined.

I was going to be with the guys tomorrow. We had planned to go to Showdown. It was a new club that one of the ex-players had opened last month in the downtown area. Females should never go to the club if they don't know the bouncer or someone that can get them in quicker than everyone else. Nothing is more attractive than seeing a group of females that walk straight into the club without waiting in line.

Along with the basic theories of mastering the game, there are also rules in which every player must follow. These rules were not designed or invented by myself, but were passed down from generation to generation. I got back to my car and just sat there for a minute. I was full and needed to go lie down. I called Tarica. She was my little cutie. She was a model and had a lot of self-esteem on the outside. On the inside she was a nervous wreck.

The last time I was over her crib she started crying about not being picked for some talent show because she was too short. Modeling was her life. She was beautiful but needed a tune-up with her heart. She had no fight. She had no idea the potential she had if she would just walk with her head up.

My Uncle Po always told me, "The game is to be told, not sold." I never understood what that meant until I realized that knowledge, and not money, was going to get me out of a lot of situations. So all I had to do was listen to stories of the old heads about how to get out of different situations. Learn the Game. The stupidest thing a person can say is, "you can't tell me I can't, when you did it." Yes they can. They can and are supposed to. If they don't then they are sinning. It's called *false teaching*.

This is a very good lesson that I learned from the old heads. Keep everything private and clean. When they talk about being clean, they are not talking about talking showers. They are talking about destroying evidence, paperwork, or anything that is tangible. Leaving behind what has been done only to be discussed between yourself and who ever you pray with.

Every female will go looking around for the key to your heart. Keep it out of reach. I left the football complex and headed to the eastside where Tarica's apartment was.

Tarica said she was watching America's Next Top Model, as usual. I had to be careful because Tarica stayed next door to another girl I was talking to. I had to park my car around the corner where my boy's apartment was.

First Golden Rule: Be aware of your surroundings and KNOW all of the players involved.

Even growing up in a big city, I still encountered situations where the six degrees of separation are always in effect. Once, I even had a situation with a mother and a daughter that got a little out of hand. I had messed with the mother first and she told me she had children my age.

I didn't believe her until I got one of her daughters pregnant. Neither found out it was by me until after she had the abortion. I showed up at the clinic, and both of them were there.

That situation was not my fault. I blame the freaky mother. The mother had like eight different baby daddies, and her daughters were freaky just like her. How was I supposed to know? Oh well.

I lay down beside Tarica and started watching some movie. I was so glad that Top Model went off. The movie had subtitles; it was like looking at a movie book, a modern day read-a-long. I was feeling comfortable and excited about the weekend to come. What I did not know is that this was the weekend that was going to change my life forever. It all started by telling Casey where I went to school.

Final Thoughts: Always be yourself, so that way if someone lies on you, no one will believe them. Words are much more than letters placed together. Words have many different meanings and can express many different thoughts. So watch your word choice. Without understanding the true meaning of the words you use, your thoughts become deficient and useless.

Chapter IV

LET'S GET IT

"If you surround yourself with negative energy, how can you expect anything postive to happen?"

Friday Morning

I ACTUALLY got up Friday morning and went to class. It was hard, but I had to do it. I was sitting on the back row of the class with my head on the wall. My eyelids felt like midgets were hanging from them. I nodded off about three times. I felt as if my head was going to roll off my neck.

The class was dim because we were looking at the projector. Two people were in consistent communication with the teacher which kept him satisfied. Since no one was in the chair in front of me, I propped my foot on the vacant chair and slumped down.

I fell asleep in about ten minutes. Like any other class, just because I went didn't mean that I had to stay. The professor talked in a monotone voice. He didn't care who was listening to him. He couldn't have. If he cared, he would have seen that he was putting half of the class was sleep. Three-fourths of the way through class, we were all sleep. I decided the best thing to do was to just leave before we got in trouble.

"Let's get it," I said as I woke up and saw everyone around me was sleep also.

It was a big lecture class so we just went out the back door. The teacher probably appreciated the fact that we left so he could have some good instructional time without us snoring or acting a fool in the back row.

Lavender filled the air as the grounds crew completed their daily work. My crew was being loud walking through campus like we usually did. We hit the corner of the building and posted up for a minute as a group of girls that were in law school passed us. Everyone started making their own catcalls as I just leaned on the wall and made eye contact with the one I wanted. She knew what time it was, and I was sure to get her later.

As they got far enough away, we started acting silly again. We formed two lines and began to set it out. We were parading around campus, "That's the sound of the man, kick back, working on the train". I don't know why, but that was our favorite chant, probably because it was the only one that everyone knew.

I had on my platinum chain which held up the platinum piece of the number seven I was wearing. It was a chick magnet that was just too big to resist. I wore jewelry to proclaim my royalty. I felt like King Tutankhamen or King Tut as most say, who had one of the most remarkable collections of gold and silver.

Yeah. Ok. The chain was a gift, but I bought the piece. I am still paying on it, but it's worth the club fame. I never dressed up for class because there wasn't anyone on campus to impress. Plus, I didn't expect to see any new faces. Just a white tee-shirt and some jean shorts will do.

We were laughing and joking as we entered the dining hall. There were only two people sitting in the far corner. The food smelled good. The crew went and got in line to eat.

"I'll be right back," I said. I had to use the bathroom, so I put my bag down by the table and went down the hall by the computer room. Then I saw a fine little red bone girl that I knew didn't attend this school sitting with her back towards me typing on the computer.

I could tell she was fine by her hair. That burnt orange, curly wet looking hair that was almost skin tone. She had the red tips on it. Not too many ugly females have hair like that, so I had to play the odds.

I rushed in the restroom to get myself together in order to approach the new chick for the first time. First impressions always count on my end. She was a prime victim of a Friday morning, and I had to make sure she saw me.

I flew into the bathroom and took the first available stall. There was no one in the bathroom. I was straining to push the urine out of my body, trying to hurry up and get back to this chick.

I shook twice, looked in the mirror, threw some water on my hands, and rushed out. The bathroom door flew open and knocked all the books and papers out of Casey's hands standing behind the entrance. A brief moment passed as we took a quick look at each other.

As our hands touched we looked at each other and started to smile. She was breaking all the rules of the pyramid by seeing me during the day but she had me enchanted for the moment.

"What are you doing up here?" I asked as we gathered her papers up off the floor.

"I had to get some information about your school for my sister. She's interested in coming next year," Casey said, showing me a brochure of the university she was placing back into her bag.

The clock tower was sounding and reminded me of where I was. It was the middle of the day on a Friday. I could not be seen talking to another girl on my campus. I had to think fast. The true test of every man is how he gets out of tight situations, seeing what was happening and understanding that everything happens for a reason. Try not to make issues your problems.

I had to get rid of Casey quick because Amber and I always meet after our eleven o'clock and get lunch in the dining hall. I had a feeling that Casey was going to ask me if I wanted to eat lunch so I had to play it cool.

"So, have you eaten already?" Casey said as we stood up and started talking.

"I'm sorry. I just ate. You should have told me you were going to be up here and we could have planned something."

"I didn't know I was coming. My sister called me this morning and said she needed this information." Her hair was covering half of her face and she had on some shades so I couldn't really see her eyes.

"Plus, you never called me back last night," she added.

"I know, I lost track of time trying to complete an assignment."

People were starting to gather by the dining hall entrance. I had to hurry up. The conversation had to end quickly before anyone of relevance showed up. We continued to look at each other in silence until another student walked by and almost bumped me. I gave her the one arm hug. That way she wouldn't make a scene in the middle of the hallway. I had to keep the party going.

The conversation was short and to the point.

"I have to run. Are we still on for tonight?" I said thinking of all the freaky things her body was telling me.

"I will call you," she said " . . . and I will definitely see you later."

I had to watch as she left out the back door to make sure she didn't run into Amber. The conversation was quick and simple but not disrespectful to the point where she would feel offended.

The game is never over; there are no time outs. As soon as you lose focus, other players gain the edge. One must always remember that there are always other players. Reading the entire playing field is a principal concept. This is where I went wrong.

Second Golden Rule: Don't talk under pressure. The wise know when not to talk. The less you talk, the less lies you tell.

WHAM! I turned around and there stood the two nosiest females on campus, Shay and Squeak. Out of the four hundred black students that attended my university, they made it their business to put everyone's business in the streets. Since they each didn't have a man, they tried to break everybody's relationship up with rumors and lies. When females aren't in a relationship they keep up more mess than a third grade snitch. I had to be wise with my words around these two.

Shay was from a small hick town outside of Chicago and was not at all attractive. Shay was a big girl and wore tight clothes. Her thighs were attached from her crouch to her knees and had to twist when she walked. She had money so the clothes were expensive but looked horrible on her.

Shay always looked like she couldn't breathe. People dealt with her mouth because her father was some rich real estate broker in Chicago, and she threw some wild parties. Everyone would dance, trash the place, and go home. She didn't care so neither did we.

Squeak was just her annoying little sidekick. That was the nickname I gave her, Sidekick. That's what I called her because that's what she was. Squeak was little and was almost hidden behind Shay. Squeak was from Mississippi and never had any money. She was country smart but knew nothing about how to interact with people. She always would have this distant look on her face.

Squeak was the only one who would put up with Shay's mouth everyday all day. It was kind of sad. Everything that Shay would say Squeak would repeat it and give you a look like as if you didn't hear her the first time.

They thought that the idea of rumors were funny and often called themselves the Queens of Gossip. If you needed to know what was going on around campus, they were the ones to ask.

They both had a million bobby pins all in their hair holding their wrap in place. It must have been an up north thing that Shay started and Squeak was just following along. I could tell because Shay's was tight and neat while Squeak's was loose and messy.

"Who was that?" they asked at the same time.

"None-ya," I stated as I turned around and tried to get as far away from them as possible.

"Who is None-ya?" Shay asked being nosey and rolling her head off her body.

"None of your business, Nose-ella," I said as I proceeded to walk back into the dining hall.

No matter how dumb you think a girl can be, there is always a way that females can prove you wrong. Shay and Squeak were two good examples of dumb-smart girls. They are very intelligent but just can't seem to grasp any common sense.

"Why don't ya'll do something with ya'll hair. That looks terrible. Which ever one of ya'll came up with that one needs to find the nearest brigde and jump," I said as I turned and started to walk away.

"Are you cheating on Amber?" Squeak asked.

"No mini-me, that was my . . . my cousin." I had to pause and think about who I was addressing.

"What school does she go to?" said Squeak.

"NYBU," I said smacking my teeth.

"What is that?" they both said together like SPEDS. For those that don't know, Speds are Special Education Students.

"None of Your Business University," I said wondering why they are asking me so many questions.

"Where is that?"

"Get out of my face," I said walking away from the conversation.

There she was. Coming around the corner was my Nubian Goddess, Amber. She was carrying two of her books close to her chest like she was cold. Her chest was fairly large so I didn't mind her walking like that. She needed to cover up in public.

Amber could really dress. She had on her little Channel outfit with the matching nap sack that was setting the tone for every girl on campus. The sun gave her skin that glow that a male is lucky to see about once or twice in his life. The glow is only a characteristic that a dime piece has. Without the glow, a dime piece cannot be truly defined as a dime piece.

"Hey baby," I said as she walked up and gave me a kiss. "How was class?"

"I see you left your class early. Again," she said, looking at me dead in my eyes to see if I was going to lie to her.

"How did you know?" I asked wondering if she saw me.

"I know because your goon squad over there is already done with their lunch. Do they have any home training?" She was trying to be funny as she looked over at the table where they were sitting, but she was right. They were eating like animals and had food all over the table.

This was the only girl with whom I thought about marriage the first time I saw her. In my studies, I found that one shouldn't sleep with a girl unless he has intensions to marry. Now whether the father allows, is on them, but I had every intent to get married at that moment.

I thought that I was tripping or something the way she made my knees buckle at first, but it is not like that any more. I make her knees buckle now, if you know what I mean. I had wanted to settle down so many times but there were issues that I had to clear up before all that could take place. Hey, I am only 19; let me live a little first.

I knew that the word was going to get around the dining hall just because Shay and Squeak were my enemies, and I knew they didn't like the way I paraded around campus. If I was caught talking to a new girl on campus, what better news to spread from the two biggest gossipers in the world? It would almost be like reaching a milestone in gossip history on this little university that was full of nerds. I could just feel everyone looking at me and Amber as we ate together.

Shay and Squeak were whispering, pointing, and looking with every conversation that they had. In order to get out of any situation, a man must tell his girl what is going on before she hears about it from the student body.

This leads us to my theory behind lies; as long as you tell her a lie before she has a chance to hear the truth, nine times out of ten, you will be ok. Even if she believes the truth it will be easier to tell her more lies that sound better and more believable. This causes confusion and doubt, which in turn causes forgetfulness along with forgiveness. Time does heal.

I learned that with my experience in the courtroom. As long as there is reasonable doubt, I can't be found guilty. Did I lose anybody? In my case, I decided to act like the surprised cousin.

"Hey, Amber," I said trying to act like I had something important to say.

"My cousin was here earlier, I wanted you to meet her."

"Who?" She asked trying to get make me say it again.

"Spanky . . . well I call her Spanky. When we were little, she was so bad she use to get a spanking every day. Her real name is Jessica." What was I talking about? I hope she believed that one.

"Well, where did she go?"

"I have no clue, something is wrong with that girl."

This short and meaningful lie saved my relationship one more day. As long as you can continue to make it to the next day, life goes on. This covered me for when her nosey friends decided to build up the courage to tell her that they think, THINK, her man is cheating on her.

From the energy in the air, I could feel the words of Shay and Squeak moving again so I decided to act on it before it was too late. I changed the subject and began asking her how her day went along with rubbing her forearm. By adding the touch, this got her focus off everything else that was going on in the lunch room. Her focus was on me now, and I had more influence on her than her friends.

The Other Side

That was close. I know it was Friday, but I had to get focused. That was just too much to start the day off. I need to do something different, go workout and relieve some stress or something. I was thinking about everything as I sat there and finished my lunch with Amber.

The lunch room was super thick and my V.I.P. corner was receiving a little more attention than I wanted. My army had taken over about six tables and had grown to now about fourty people. We were all tight in a little corner and the males surrounded the females that were already sitting down. Territorial style.

I gave Amber a kiss and headed out the back with Keith. "Bout to go, give me a kiss," I said leaving still the love of her life.

Keith was a year older than I. We were basically brothers. Keith's parent would often go through difficult times and he would spend weeks at my house. We went to the same high school and everything. He helped me get into school up here after he balled out his freshmen year. Now he can do whatever he wants to.

He told the coach that he needed to fill the team with people from his high school because we breed athletes at my high school. Keith and I were supposed to be roommates, but he got permission to stay off-campus because he was taking care of a child. He and his girl live together in a nice apartment that the school was paying for. As long as he kept doing his thing on the field, he was going to the league.

We headed towards the football practice facility. I was calm and collected around school but a ruthless and mean tyrant when it came to football. I couldn't live life knowing that someone was more physically capable of doing something better than me.

We got over to the football complex and went separate ways. Keith had to check some academic stuff, so he went straight into the academic support center. I, on the other hand, wasn't trying to see anyone. I went straight to the locker room to chill out.

Our complex was state-of-the-art. We had TVs in each locker and machines that I had no clue how to work. The locker room was most of the guys second home away from the dorm room. People would often sleep in the locker room during classes instead of walking all the way back to their rooms.

The concept of a locker room is almost like having a safe haven to speak on certain issues. The locker room was a place where men can talk amongst each other and not have it leak out to the streets. But like any other case, there were always haters.

Our locker room had one guy in particular. He was not allowed to sit around and listen anymore because we found out last week he let something that was shared amongst the locker room get out. He could not even sit around and laugh at everything due to the fact that he was considered lame now by the upperclassmen. What made it so bad is that he was my suitemate, Mickey's roommate.

Bruce played wide receiver, so we went against each other everyday in practice. He grew up about thirty minutes outside my city so we kind of represent the same hoods. He stayed within the metropolitan area.

Bruce had a girlfriend, Jamie, but was trying to be a player at the same time. He was one of those guys that you could tell was acting out of character most of the time. He was learning the game, but there was still a lot he did not understand. I felt like it was kind of my responsibility to show him the ropes since we shared the same room and all. I had to so he wouldn't mess up my game.

Bruce and I came on our official visit together. I was fly, but Bruce was dressed like a person trying to represent what city he was from. He was so lame he would embroider all of his hats with his nickname: Young Frezze. I don't know who told him that was cool. I was always taught not to put my name on my clothes because then strangers can acted like they knew you. He had one outfit that had his name on his hat, shirt, and shoes. So lame.

See, Bruce was cool with everyone until he started telling his girlfriend and other females what we said. I never knew if he was trying to get with a certain girl or just being a hater out of pure jealously. Maybe he was telling his girl in order to feel important, like he was cool or something and hangs with the rest of the guys. This was his boost of confidence with his girl.

"What it do?" Bruce said as he entered the locker room.

"Shut up lame," Keith said as he entered right behind Bruce. Keith really didn't like him.

"And take your arms out of your shirt. You look like a little girl." Bruce had both his arms in his shirt like he was cold. Keith would call him out on everything that he would do.

I knew that I had to keep my haters closer than my friends. That's the only reason I wasn't so direct with my words. I was calmer than Keith. I just have a quiet barrier that I put up whenever Bruce comes around. I knew I had to watch him. It was funny because as soon as I met Bruce this summer, he tried my gangster. What he did was so stupid I knew he was lame after that.

See, one of my former girlfriends decided to visit one of the weekends that Amber didn't come in the summer. We were in summer practice, and there weren't any females on campus so I had to import mine. I was messing around, and Tiffany knew it. We weren't together anymore.

I was having relations with her and one of her friends. They both knew it but had to live with the fact they both still wanted me. I wasn't tripping. I considered them to be a tag team.

Both of them were in the rotation but emotions started to take place. She was so dingy that she didn't find out until she reached the city because she was on the phone telling the girl she was coming to see me. Emotions got involved, and the truth came out. Pressure busts pipes.

Well the story goes as this. Tiffany drove all the way to see me. She then decides that she is going to turn around and leave because I had an event to attend and couldn't see her until later. She was going to have to wait.

I was really going to see this chick that I had met earlier that day, but she didn't need to know that. I mean, she was crying and all that other girl stuff.

"I hate you," she'd even said to me. Walking out of the room just to come back in and say something else about why she shouldn't be with me. Eventually, I left her in the room by herself. This is when Bruce decided to take his shot.

"You know that he isn't going to change . . . it's college. If you need somewhere to sleep tonight you can stay in my room. Just let me know," he said to Tiffany.

He didn't know who I was at the time. I suppose that's why he tried me like that. Would somebody tell him that we are suitemates and that we sleep basically in the same room? Only sheetrock separates us. I mean some girls might fall for that weak line but this one had a little common sense. To make things worse for him, she told me right after it happened. This only brought us closer together. She believed in loyalty not love. He thought he could play on the fact that she was emotional. She was mad, not stupid, at this point.

Ever since then, I haven't missed one opportunity to let him know that he can't beat me at anything. He should have known that I got the magic stick, for real. It's all tied into the Three-Point Star Theory, and she knew she had to be loyal. He really just made my night that much better because it went from a one hitter quitter to a double header.

Keith and I sat there getting ready for practice and watching TV. I could tell that something was wrong with Keith, but I let it slide because I knew if it was serious then he would tell me.

"Coach in the locker room," one of the big defensive linemen called out as our strength coach came in with good news.

"Just helmets . . . just helmets," he said leaving so quickly that everyone else had to repeat it.

I already had on my shorts so I was straight. Everyone else was acting crazy throwing their football pants on top of the locker as if it was a joyful occasion. To not have a full practice was like preparing your mouth for a hot dog and getting a steak.

This was big. It was Friday, and everyone was trying to go out. Since practice was going to be short, that meant no one was going to be tired. The night was going to be wild.

Mr. Nosey

We took the field to practice the same time we did everyday, 2:45 p.m. We only had fourteen periods since it was Friday, and the first game wasn't until next weekend.

"I see ya Big Keith!" I yelled out across the field to wake everyone up.

"I see ya Double Dog!" that was what Keith called me, because he said I was double the dog that everyone else was.

I hated stretching so I just sat there and talked about everybody for fifteen minutes until they were ready to start. I told ya'll I was a Blue Chip athlete. I did what I wanted to.

Something was bothering me about how happy this clown Bruce was about tonight. I even once heard him make a long sinister laugh. I wasn't scared of life. I was open to whatever the night had to bring.

Eventually, I had to tell Bruce to calm down. He was acting like a virgin and was going to scare the female away. Immaturity is very noticeable around older women. Mentally a man has to be in control over his actions in order for a mature woman to respect him. Maturity is what he didn't have.

I participated in walk through but stood there while the team did a couple of sprints for conditioning. My ankle was still bothering me so I stayed clear of all the unnecessary running the team was doing. The sky was clear as I just lay there. Two helicopters were flying above.

"Nothing but ghetto birds," I said to one of the trainers that had no clue as to what I was talking about. Practice was over and I went into the locker room and started talking to Keith. We were talking about all kind of stuff. I remembered that I had bumped into Casey earlier, so we got on that subject.

"Shawty, that girl came up here," I told Keith

"Who?" he replied.

"That girl, Casey," Keith had a look on his face like he didn't know her.

"I've never seen her before, have I?" Keith asked trying to remember.

"I met this one at NV Tuesday. That's what I meant to ask you," I had to think about that night. "Where did you go anyways?

Some random girl brought me back to the room and was just sitting there starring at me."

"You don't remember?" he asked as he started laughing.

"I was drinking a lot."

"You don't remember that girl following you into the bathroom." He was laughing harder now.

"I don't know what happened to you. All I know is that she went into the stall with you and ya'll were in there for about thirty minutes." He was almost choking at this point.

"Was she cute?" I had to know that.

"She was finer than a lil bit. But . . ." he started rolling on the ground.

"What Man?"

"I think that she only had one leg . . . hahhaha."

"Ah man. I think I do remember now!"

We sat there laughing for a minute as I began to remember. She did have one leg. I was just too sick to care about something like that at the time. We were both on the floor by now. Tears were coming out of Keith's eyes because he was laughing so hard. We looked up and Bruce was there.

"What's so funny?" Bruce said starting to laugh just because.

"Like we going to tell you. You lucky you got a pass over here. I should make you go back to your side," Keith said as he gathered himself back in his locker and wiped his face.

I hated the fact that I needed Bruce to wake me up every morning. I was not a morning person, and Bruce would be up at six every morning. I didn't have to hang with him, but he was a good alarm clock. I kind of felt like a big brother or a role model to him. That was no excuse for some of the things that he would do. Next thing I know, here comes Bruce asking a question.

"So, where ya'll going tonight?" said Bruce.

"To Showdown." Showdown was the newest club on the Westside that one of the former football players had just opened, so we were VIP.

"I'm going . . . if that's cool with ya'll."

Bruce was always good for inviting himself everywhere. If I would have said NO, then he was going to ask, why not. Then I would have to hear about it back in the room. If I say yes he is going to ask about some girl. What did I do? I said yes.

"Yeah, man."

Keith just looked at me because he knew where the conversation was going. Then it came.

"I saw that girl you were wit outside the bathroom. You got all the females man. Let me borrow one for the night?"

I knew that was coming. Did everybody see me talking to Casey? I have got to be more careful with whom I'm seen with in public.

"That wasn't me. I don't know what your talking about." I always said "it wasn't me" just because I never believe in self-incrimination. There was no telling who he would tell.

"Well if that wasn't you then let me tell you, it was this fine girl in the café today. She had burnt org . . ."

"Shut up. That was me." I had to stop him or he would have went on for days about some girl he could have almost met.

"That is a BET!" Bruce said.

Along with knowing my surroundings, the third golden rule has to deal with the company you keep. My Third Golden Rule is kind of tricky because you never really know the true intentions of anyone-listen when I say anyone—around you. Haters don't disappear and hatred can take over envious eyes. Keeping your eye on your haters is completely different from hanging with them. Haters only hate. They don't participate or congratulate. They just hate.

My Third Golden Rule allows you to kind of see who is really loyal. If you can notice something that isn't right, everyone that knows you should know that it isn't right for you. In saying that, one must keep consistent communication with his most respected friend. Notice I didn't use the word trust, for trust will get you killed. Respect changes from situation to situation. With the Third Golden Rule one must go to the wisest person in the situation.

Third Golden Rule: When you venture into distant lands travel in pairs of two, for everyone does not play a fair game and a true companion will aide you through rough times.

Allowing Bruce to go with us was a little stupid. I knew it, but Keith was going to be there, and I respected him to the utmost degree. Plus, I'm a cowboy and like a good challenge.

Any time you mix loud males and females cows, there is no way that you can have a fun time. The loud male is going to hate if no one in the group of females wants to talk to him, causing him to become louder and even obnoxious. That messes up the night for every other male in the group. A bad apple can ruin the entire bunch. Remember that. I was going to have a close eye on everything in order for it to run smoothly.

Practice was only one hour, but it felt like five. Before I left the locker room, I decided to call the main, Amber.

"You cooked?" I had to ask. I was hungrier than two thick girls leaving Bally's.

"I will. What do you want?"

"Surprise me with your best dish, something you know I would like," I said with a French accent. Plus, I was seeing if she knew what I liked.

"Ok, I'll call you when it's ready."

By this I could accomplish two things that were very important in maintaining a healthy relationship. First, I had made sure she knew I was thinking about her when I was with my friends.

Secondly, I had to find out where she was going to be. That way we wouldn't meet up unexpectedly. I was going to eat and then tuck her in so I could go out.

Being with your girlfriend in a public place is something that I did not approve of at this point in my life: the mall, movies, or Wal-Mart are different. Going to the club with your girl should be a sin and outlawed by the government. That is asking for a fight. Your girl should never be mad at who you are with in public, but focus on who you are with in privacy. If you want to keep a man, don't let him sleep alone.

I just think there are too many lames in the club that bring their main girl. When someone touches your girl on her butt then you're ready to fight. If the President really wanted to stop the violence, he would ban males from bringing their girls to the club. They should only be for the singles or singles at heart. Unless you had a VIP booth and ballin, don't walk around the dance floor holding your girls hand. If you have to bring her, either get a booth or sit at the bar.

The conversation between Amber and I lasted about ten to fifteen minutes. Remembering that even though she is my girl, I still paid the phone bill. Now if she wanted to pay, then I could talk to her all day. She doesn't, so I don't.

This was a good conversation to me. The call was informational as well as meaningful, and takes no real time away from the day. I am off the phone, and I have all of my plans for the night in order. This cuts down on my phone minutes, and everyone in the situation is happy. I would rather go buy a new outfit then pay an expensive phone bill.

Final Thoughts: "You can't play the game if you don't know the rules. Otherwise the people that know the rules will manipulate them in order to win every time. If you live by the simplest laws, all other laws don't matter."

(Insert)

Logically Thinking:

In my reading to comprehend, Willie Lynch was not an advocate of hanging black people. He focused on the idea that if he could separate the black male and female mentally, then it would be hundreds of years before we would realize we were fighting against each other. The goal was to keep the black male physically strong but mentally weak, as well as keeping the black female physically weak and mentally independent. We have to break this cycle. The black men needs to become more mentally strong. Our black women, for a change, need to stand behind us in support. I'm not saying for the women to fall back; we need them to remain strong. I'm suggesting help. Help us help each other. We are a race of many different shades, cultures, and traditions. We will never be on the same accord in that aspect. That doesn't mean that we can't still sing together and make beautiful music. Let's not try to synthesize but harmonize because within harmony comes peace.

Excerpts from the Willie Lynch Speech:
(www.thetalkingdrum.com)

"Understanding is the best thing. Therefore, we shall go deeper into this area of the subject matter concerning what we have produced here in this breaking process of the female nigger. We have reversed the relationship; in her natural uncivilized state, she would have a strong dependency on the uncivilized nigger male, and she would have a limited protective tendency toward her independent male offspring and would raise male offsprings to be dependent like her."

"In this frozen, psychological state of independence, she will raise her MALE and female offspring in reversed roles. For FEAR of the young male's life, she will psychologically train him to be MENTALLY WEAK and DEPENDENT, but PHYSICALLY STRONG. Because she has become psychologically independent, she will train her FEMALE offsprings to be psychologically independent. What have you got? You've got the nigger WOMAN OUT FRONT AND THE nigger MAN BEHIND AND SCARED."

"Furthermore, we talked about paying particular attention to the female savage and her offspring for orderly future planning. Then more recently we stated that, by reversing the positions of the male and female savages, we created an orbiting cycle that turns on its own axis forever unless a phenomenon occurred and reshifts positions of the male and female savages"

"You know language is a peculiar institution. It leads to the heart of a people. The more a foreigner knows about the language of another country the more he is able to move through all levels of that society. Therefore, if the foreigner is an enemy of the country, to the extent that he knows the body of the language, to that extent is the country vulnerable to attack or invasion of a foreign culture. For example, if you take a slave, if you teach him all about your language, he will know all your secrets, and he is then no more a slave, for you can't fool him any longer, and BEING A FOOL IS ONE OF THE BASIC INGREDIENTS OF ANY INCIDENTS TO THE MAINTENANCE OF THE SLAVERY SYSTEM."

Willie Lynch

Chapter V

GAME TIME

"Human nature is a natural hater so tighten up your circle. Keep loyal lions close, and remember that monkeys in gorilla suits will hurt ya."

I'm Ready

AFTER my conversation with Amber, I picked myself up something quick to eat and headed back to the room. Shawty was already there when I arrived. Shawty was my roommate. His real name was Kenny, but he was only five foot two so we called him Shawty.

Shawty was also from my city and all he knew was how to party. He went to a private high school back home. His school was only for people that had big money. He didn't play football and didn't want to play football. The only weight he lifted was in Ziploc bags.

Shawty and Keith were in the room getting dressed. Since Keith didn't live on the campus he would often use our room to change clothes whenever we would go out.

"Let me wear these ones tonight," Shawty said, looking at my Prada shades.

"I haven't even worn them yet." I could tell that he had already tried them on because they weren't in the same place I'd left them.

"So are you wearing them tonight?" he asked trying to corner me into letting him wear them.

"Yeah," I responded quickly.

"I know you're lying but it's cool, I will just wear your Polo's then."

"Don't you have a pair?"

"Yeah, but I like yours better. They look more expensive," he said looking in the mirror at himself.

"That's because they are, cheap self."

If they were getting dressed, then I knew that I had about an hour to eat before I had to start to get ready. We were all crew and all, but it takes them entirely too long to get ready to go anywhere: getting daily shape-ups, cleaning their shoes, ironing their clothes, and putting on jewelry. All that stuff that normal males try to do, we do to perfection. We had an image to keep. Some would call us "Ballers". It paid off with the amount of women that came through.

Me and my boys stayed clean. We all felt as if we had a place in society and had a lot of pride in how we looked when we went out in public. We are not Kappa's or anything. In fact, we gave those Kappa's a run for their money. We stay clean for a bunch of football players. We played all of the skilled positions on the football field anyways so the spotlight was mostly on us. We had great stage presence. We left being big and ugly to the linemen since most of them were Q-Dogs. Being a clean and well-dressed male is an image that every man should try to achieve.

Going back in history, the most powerful men dressed in royal garments and presented himself as a high person in society. Look at some of the great pharaohs like King Khaba, King Snefru, or King Khurfu. These great Kings dressed in all types of royal garments. No one could see the King unless he was properly dressed.

Most of the great King's daily routine was spent getting ready. The proper bathing, grooming, and clothing had to be handled in a certain manner that was fit for royalty. I considered my crew the royal court.

It doesn't take me take long to get dressed because most of my things are new and don't need ironing. For Keith and Shawty, it took about an hour to get ready to go anywhere. Everyone had to be fresh with some kind of gear on in order to get in my ride. Everyone clean, plus driving a clean ride equals success.

I thought we were in the clear as we walked down the steps to the first floor when my phone rang.

"Hey man, what time are ya'll going?" It was Bruce.

"Man, we leaving now," I said hoping he was going to say that he couldn't go because he was studying or something.

"I'll be outside the dorm in five. My girl had to go somewhere real quick," he said happily.

"Aight man, hurry up."

That was kind of a good move to wait because we needed the extra car. Bruce is the only one with a ride except me. If he wasn't going then Keith would have had to drive. That means that we would have to walk three blocks because Keith don't let nobody see his car. It is a red, green, and blue 79 Pinto. When I say a lemon, I mean lemon. It reminds me of Red's car on the movie Friday. Well, Keith's Pinto is worse than that. We stayed in constant fear that the car was going to blow up on us one day if someone hit us from the rear.

Keith was always quick to put a sound system in his car. The whole back seat might be a big speaker. He would always say that his car was like a person. The only thing that counts is the inside. That was the lamest thing I have ever heard. Keith promises to get a new car when he gets to the league.

And it's on

We ran into some chicks on the way out the door and stopped to talk for a minute. Big Boi, one of our defensive linemen, told Bruce that he was driving his girl's car so he had to get in the back seat with us. The whole time we were in the car Keith was clowning on Bruce. He even got sensitive on one joke which made everyone get on him even harder. Nothing is funnier than joking on a sensitive male. You will never run out of things to say because everything gets on a sensitive male's nerves.

We drove around for five minutes so everyone could see my new Expedition truck. Ken, the owner of the club, was going to let us in free. We just had to call ahead of time and let him know what time to look out for us. I called as soon as we got off the highway. Ken usually cut off his phone because he said everyone would start calling as soon as the club opened. That was his way of hiding out. He was a real player type of guy, and that's why I messed with him.

We already had our entrance plan that we used every time we went out. First, we had to get in the regular line to make it seem like we were regular. Then we would say, "This line is too long, we ain't waiting in no line," and being loud about it. As we got out of the regular line, we would grab about three or four girls and walk in through the VIP Line.

We pulled up to the valet and hopped out in front of everyone. The way it was set up was perfect because the regular line was right in front of us. We stood there for a moment then proceeded with the plan.

"You comin'?" Shawty asked a cute girl that noticed we were going to the VIP Line.

"I'm with her," she responded as she looked at her ugly friend.

"I guess not . . . dang girl. You ain't got no cute friends? She looks more like your pet. Well I guess you are cute enough for the both of ya. Come on." This boy was stupid and didn't care about offending anybody.

This gives us a little clout when people saw us in the club. This childish act gave us a kick to start the night off. It was fun and really didn't make sense. I guess that's why we did it. We would be known as the baller outside that paid for about ten people. When no one really knew that we got in for free.

The club was crunk outside. It had to be two hundred people outside and it was only about 11:30. As we headed up to the door, I was leading the pack. My piece and chain were blinging, fresh pair of air forces with the fresh outfit that was right out of the store. Everything was clean and moving in the right direction.

As we reached the VIP Line, I saw this thick girl. I couldn't really see her face, but from behind I could tell who she was. It was only one person like that walking around here. So I walk up on her and whisper in her ear.

"Don't I know you from somewhere?" I asked gripping her waist and pulled her close to me.

She replied without turning around, "From where?"

"From my fantasy last night," I released my grip as she turned around with a smile on her face.

"You so crazy, boy," Casey was still fashionably correct with her shades. It was something about those shades that kept turning me on.

After doing the whole introduction of her friends and mine, everyone became a little more comfortable. Being the alpha male in this situation I had to remember that proper introductions must be done to take ones' self out of the equation of being a hater. This is a very key moment in meeting friends. If you don't introduce common friends it seems as if you are mocking the sly and boasting the humble.

It got to the point where I could not wait until the party was over. Those tight black pants had me going crazy. All I was focused on was those legs, cute booty, and that little waist. Everyone had their eyes on her, and she had her eyes on me. At this point, I lost all logic and almost began to stare at her butt. Then she asked me, "How much is it?"

"Don't ask questions like that. You with me tonight," I was smooth with mine. She knew what time it was and wasn't tripping at all.

She was looking like she was going to be ready for seduction later so I wasn't tripping either. I always considered myself to be among the highly educated, so I could only imagine what a female like this could do to a male that had no self confidence. Now I see why some cute girls are dating ugly guys. They can enchant them into doing whatever they want.

"That's a big butt," Shawty said as he bumped into me as we entered the foyer area of the club.

"I know. She knows I'm looking, too."

"I see ya killa," Shawty said, as he showed admiration to my game.

"We're here with Big Dog," I told one of the bouncers that was checking IDs.

"Who?"

"Big Dog. Ken-the Owner." He didn't know anyone. He just worked here. He had no clue who anyone was. He had no rank so conversation was pointless.

I looked passed him and started using hand signals to get Ken's attention because he was standing in the doorway. We were good. Forget the outside. It was jumping on the inside. The ladies were out. The bar was super thick, and they were doing some new two-step on the dance floor.

The club had three floors and had different music playing on each floor. We entered from the street level, which was the second floor. Downstairs was for the younger crowd. The club was 18 and up, most of the freshmen were down stairs dancing wild. The DJ only played down south music and kept it crunk the whole night. Everyone was sweating downstairs and didn't care. It felt a "Year of Release" party. The main floor was for the up-north crowd, mostly

Roca-fella or Dipset fans: everyone thinking that they are from New York, walking around with big hats and little heads. The top floor was Reggae, Reggae-Ton, Salsa, and Bacatra music. This is where all the bad females that could dance were.

Everyone that had fake IDs went straight to the bar and started buying beer. Beer was the cheapest thing to buy and would get you right.

"Let me get seven Buds and . . . what's your drink special?"

"We got two for one tonight on all mixed drinks."

"Well let me get two vodka and cranberry, four long islands top shelf, and four Patron Margaritas." I got my Pell-Grant this morning as I went by the financial aid office, so I had to show off a little.

Casey said that she didn't drink, but I still sat one of the Margaritas next to her arm that was resting on the bar. I looked away as if not to notice her taking a sip. After about two or three minutes I left the bar.

"I'll be right back," I said. I had to walk around and let everyone know that I was in the building.

I was a neighborhood superstar already in the city with the locals. I knew everyone from the lowest of the lames, to the crunkest of the cool people, from party thrower to class *go-ers*, from every salutatorian to every slut. Walking around the club was like a fashion show. All the ladies were dressed to impress. I could tell the scary males because they were too intimidated to approach the females. Not me. I got two new numbers in my first lap around each floor.

As I made it back to the bar I regained focus on what was really at hand. Casey. Keith and Shawty were still at the bar talking and doing what they do. They knew my nightly goal, so they already knew what time it was when I gave them the *I'm about to go, she's ready* head nod. I knew Casey was ready to leave because I noticed that the drink I left for her was empty. I was feeling good as well because everyone was passing me drinks as I was walking through the club.

Casey gave me a look and then whispered those words that I don't think that any man can resist. "Let's go to your car. I have something to show you."

Everyone knew what we were going to do. Well, I know one thing I wasn't thinking about how silly I looked when I was jumping over that pole and almost busted my butt in front of everybody. Yeah, I almost fell in front of the whole line, but I caught myself and was able to play it off smooth. I don't think that anyone even noticed. Plus, I was drinking, so embarrassment was the last thing that was on my mind, even though I did scuff up my air forces. Casey thought that it was cute. She felt that I had a sense of humor. I think.

She was laughing, and for kind of a long time now since I'm thinking about it. Maybe she did not think that it was cute and was just laughing because it was funny that I almost fell. I'm going to see if she is laughing when we get to the car.

Oh well. I wasn't thinking about none of that during the walk toward my truck as I laughed at all the busters that were still in line. Casey was doing her thang. She was walking like one of those girls in the movies that are in front of a wind blower. Well this wasn't a movie, it was just a little windy outside. She had to have Indian in her family because a real black girl would need a lot of gel to make her hair look like this. I just wanted to pet her like she was a wild cheetah with the way her hair laid down in the back.

The doors unlocked on the car. *Bup-Bup.* I love making that noise when I open the car doors; it made me feel important and up on my car game. I knew to only leave my key for the valet but keep my control pad. If someone were to get to shooting, all those people that parked valet would be dead. The automatic starter really set the tone as we climbed in and the music was already playing.

Casey and I sat there for about one minute, at the most. We were trying to hold small talk about school.

"Sooo . . . . . what are you studying?" I asked.

"I don't know yet. I haven't declared a major." Well since she didn't know what she wanted to do in school there wasn't any reason to talk about it. I was trying to make small talk, but it was not working.

Her hair was wet and curly like she was a mermaid emerging out of the water. The light from the sunroof gave her body a shine that not even the color wheel could describe: a bronze and gold combination that was radiant. The energy grew. I don't think that either of us could wait any longer. One last look at each other, and it was murder he wrote.

We attacked each other like we were wild animals. I was biting her shirt. She took her tights off before she climbed on top of me. Her booty was gripped by the palms of my hands. We were like lions pouncing on our prey.

Her bra laced my windows like drapes in a room. Her thighs were so juicy. They felt like melting butterscotch as the vent was warming her backside on my dashboard. The temperature rose to around 96 degrees, and we were both dressed in our birthday suits. We moved around until we found the right position. I knew when I found it because she clenched up in efforts of holding on.

"Do me," she groaned as she bit into my ear. This was that passionate, back scratching, juices flowing, moaning and groaning type of relations that every man dreams about. As I reclined my seat, Casey began to reach a climax as she felt more of me inside of her.

"Oh baby," she yelled as I covered her mouth with my shoulder.

"Oh baby," she kept repeating as she bit into my flesh which made the pleasure and pain equal.

Forty-five minutes had passed and she had got hers for the third time. I was ready. The taste of strawberries and Him cologne filled the truck and fogged the windows with passion. I turned her around.

I wanted this moment to last throughout the night, but she was starting to dry out. I can't stand when females dry out before I get mine. Two warm bodies rubbing naked against one another is the best feeling in the world. If I don't get what I came for then it would be a waste of a good time.

"Grab the wheel," I commanded as I put her head between her legs and her hands on the stirring wheel. "Now you drive," I said as she went wild, bouncing up and down out of control. As people would walk by, we would pause and giggle not to make to much noise. I even think that one guy was looking through the window for about five minutes without us knowing.

Everything was going great, the relations, the mood, and the excitement of being caught.

"Hold on," I said as I felt myself stiffen. By this time, I was taking the lead and she was hitting the roof of the truck as I kept throwing her up and catching her as she came down. I didn't want to see her face. Just backside everywhere.

My hands gripped her butt, and I held it where it was. I slowed down and took my time as my toes got tight, and my muscles were hardened all through my body. Then I became relaxed as it felt like all my energy was passed to her. She was out.

That was the fun part and that was over. She laid on me until I made the first move to grab my shorts. We started putting on our clothes to head back into the club. I always keep baby wipes and cologne in the glove compartment just for special occasions like this. Everything was going good, and then she had to go and say it. These words will haunt a man for the rest of his life.

"I never thought that my first time would be like this," she said as she took a deep breath and threw her head back in exhaustion.

"*Ain't no way she just said that.*" I didn't say that out loud, but that is what was going through my head at the time.

No, No, No!

The car was quiet, and I wasn't saying anything. Casey was putting on her clothes, and I was just thinking about what she just told me. Why would she lie? I knew what type of girl she was, but she expected me to believe her.

Oh, so now she is a Virgin, America. After all of that, she wants to tell me that she is a virgin. That means that I am going to have that virgin attachment on my shoulders now. Girls tend to compare or either try and hold on to their first sexual encounter, if it's good, and I am. That's why, I DON'T LIKE VIRGINS.

I mean there is nothing wrong with being a virgin. Just don't let me know. Then to prove my point just listen to what happened next.

"You lying?" were the first words that came out of my mouth.

"Lying about what?" she answered acting as if her remarks weren't out of the ordinary.

"This was your first time?"

"Yeah . . . why . . . you think I'm out there like that? Is that why you tried me?"

"It's just that . . . well . . . I ain't tripping."

I didn't know what to say at the time, so I didn't say anything.

"So what are you doing tomorrow?" I said trying to get rid of her.

"Nothing. Why?" she said trying to be seductive as if she was ready for another round of pleasure.

"I was going to try and catch up wit you whenever you got up," I said trying to get over the part about her being a virgin.

"Well I will be there when you get up so we will discuss that then," she said with a devious look on her face.

My mom told me that cute girls weren't "nothing but trouble". Did I listen? NO. Now I have a crazy, want to be virgin, crab, crazy chicken-head that wants to spend the night in my dorm room. No, no, no!

First, we have to understand what type of guy I am. I had a complete different mentality from being a pimp, a player, or a committed man. I am all three put into one, depending on the situation. I call it a master of the game. In this situation I had to think.

I watched Casey as she straightened up her hair and threw her shades back on. The air in the truck grew still. I wanted to lash out at her, but that wouldn't make any sense. What was known didn't have to be said. I allowed my actions to speak for me. She tried to grab my hand, and I acted as if I was looking for my shoe. I didn't want her to touch me. She had moved from a lady to a cow.

The Rules of the Sleeping Over differentiate based on the types of people (players). Each kind of male has a different set of rules for having a female sleep over. For example, the traditional Pimp does not have a pyramid. He treats all females the same, even his mom. His whole intensions are to get money from females. He doesn't really want to work for money. What does he do to get money? He uses his ability to get females to do it for him.

Fine, short, tall, black, yellow, it does not matter to a Pimp. As long as he gets something from that female, she is welcome to be in his presence. When it comes to sleeping in his room, a Pimp might sleep with two, three, or four girls at the same time. The key to a Pimp is that he allows everyone in the situation to know that he is the Pimp.

The second type of person that one could encounter is a Player. A Player has the pyramid in which I talked about earlier. Players are the smart, educated, cute, brothers that think they are gods-gift to women. A Player is never satisfied.

See everyone thinks that a Player does not get caught up in the game. NOT TRUE. A player gets caught up the most; it is how he deals with the issues that differentiate him from others. Charm and wisdom are key. A Player's motivation is that he might get caught: living on the edge, always wanting to be seen, going further and beyond the call of duty.

Yeah, when that quiet cute boy is sitting in the corners don't think that he is quiet or shy. He is plotting and coming up with a strategy of how to avoid conflict while still talking to the other three girls in the club.

I will tell you a secret. This is one of my favorite lines. If a guy tells you that he does not like to talk to girls in the club and that would rather get to know them outside of the club setting, then he has other girls in the same place and is trying to get rid of you as quickly as possible. That always works because most females are bold enough to talk to someone in front of their male friend. Why did I tell ya'll that? Well, like I said earlier the game is to be told not sold. Take it and run with it!

Then there is the committed male. I don't know what to tell ya'll. Your girl is probably committed to you because of a guy like me. A prime example was Bruce. He was someone who had finally found a woman but felt as if he still could play the relationship game. He dosen't know how to play but tries since he is now forced to at-tempt to gain the upper hand in his own relationship.

I got out of the car and opened the back door. My shirt had made it all the way to the speakers. She was sitting there watch-ing me as I threw just one of my sleeves on. I had on my tank top. I wasn't completely naked but I was trying to show off the little work I put into the weight room.

The VIP Lot had a couple people walking around. As I lit one up, Casey gave me a look. She wanted to hit it. I didn't offer her a hit cause that would have been creating a completely different beast.

My *Acting Right theory*: a basic theory that goes way back. You can't trust any female! It's not that you can't trust anybody; it's the fact you can't trust any female. No matter what I did at this moment, she was ready to ride. The smoke haze blocked my vision of her and gave me time to think before I reacted. The situation was common, and there were many different ways I could have approached it. I mean there are some exceptions to this situation like Nuns and Amish women. They don't really count. I even know a couple of Nuns that didn't obey all their relationship qualifications. The main one being, *No relations without marrige* sounds a little dumb to me.

I turned the music down to let her know I was about to head back inside. "Ready?" I asked. I didn't even want to be seen with her at this moment. I saw her as a different person. It felt as if I had been in this situation one too many times: nice and attractive female, and that's all. There was nothing else. Then Casey probably had some other guy waiting on her, pacing around the floor, wondering if she was alright back in the club. She couldn't play me.

I'm saying that men who think that their females are faithful were either deprived as a child, ugly as a child, or have low self-esteem due to issues that I don't want to embarrass anyone with (you know what I mean, packing a snack, not a meal). Any girl looking for the perfect man, you better call Dionne Warrick or Ms. Cleo because I can't help you.

Looking for love? Love.com has free membership. I see it as this, I am 19 years old now, and the life expectancy for males is 80. That's 61 years; that's a long time with one person. There is no need for me to rush. That's why there are so many divorcees and little bastard children running around. Stop using love as an outlet to fullfill the pleasure of having relations. If you don't take a minute to wrap it up, you will be spending years dishing it out. Its not how much love you have, it's how much money you have that counts.

Ya'll see the problem with Casey spending the night. If she was trying to get back to the room she should have never done it in the car. Now she is considered a truck chick and not a chick. Anytime I wanted to do something freaky in my truck this is who I'm going to call. She ain't never got to even see my room.

Usually "the dog goes away to play, but comes back home to lay," and lay I did, with Amber. Every night, no matter what time it was, I would go stay a couple of hours. I was switching from my player role to my committed role. Only real masters of the game truly understand how to accomplish this.

As I closed the door, Casey tried to grab my hand again to solidify that we were together: not going to happen. I looked at her.

"Don't be trying to hold my hand on the sly." I said it in a joke, but I was dead serious. "Your man might be watching," I continued.

"You scared of a little competition?" she said as she smiled back at me, now grabbing my whole arm.

"Competition? Do you know who I am? Ain't no competition! I just don't want you to get your tail whooped when you get home."

"By who?" Casey said shocked, as if it couldn't happen.

"I don't know. I ain't taking no chances, either. Now let me go." I broke away from her grip and slid my hand down to hers. We locked pinky fingers for about ten more steps before completely releasing each other. I was still player with it.

The club was still jumping, but I had accomplished what I came for. I was going to get me another drink then I was going to be ready to go.

I had to at least go by Amber's room. Amber always wanted me to come over her room after I had been out just to make sure I'm not out drunk and driving around causing trouble. I really think that she wanted to make sure that I was not sleeping with any other girl. It's a little too late for that. So, what do I do?

I'm smart. THINK. Ok. I got it. I am going to make this a group activity. See, if anything goes wrong when you are with other people, you can always put the blame on someone that is lame. Well not lame, but just another person that wouldn't mess up what I had worked so hard to build. So I came up with a fool-proof plan.

I was going to get Casey and her friends to come up to the room with Bruce and the other guys. This way they will be occupied with all of my boys flirting with her friends. I know they will. I will then be able to sneak out, turn off my phone, and go to Amber's room.

I will probably give Casey a reason tomorrow like, "I had to go help someone that was in trouble, and my phone went dead." A girl can't argue with a male that is going to help a friend that's in trouble. If she does, that is automatic grounds for dismissal. She won't risk that. I mean this was guaranteed. I planned it, so it had to work. It had worked many times in the past, and it was for sho' to work.

We walked back into the club as we showed the bouncer our V.I.P. bands. He remembered our faces and wasn't trippin'. I went straight to the bar, and Casey was right behind me. We were attached at the hip. Her hand was in my pocket. I couldn't go anywhere without her. I stood by the bar and got another drink. Casey was straight and was starting to get ready for another round.

"You ready?" Casey asked.

"I see you are," I replied as I could feel her hand unzipping my pants at the bar.

We were facing each other so no one could see what she was doing. Her hand found its way into my pants. I was ready now. I had to find everyone so I could get out of here.

Final Thoughts: Recognition and comprehension is only half the battle. The execution occurs when a man is sent to fulfill a man's job. If you're not mentally here, then you're not here at all.

Chapter VI

Come On Now

"If you believe everything that everyone says, you'll be messed up. Stop listening to lies because everyone tells them. Believe in what is written down and verified, for words are intangible and rely on human nature for its existence."
—CHAI

Not So Fast!!

It was about three o'clock in the morning and the club was closing in thirty minutes. The lights were starting to come on, and the social groups were party-hopping around doing their social calls. I found Keith and Shawty talking to two females on the top floor. I wasn't going to hate, so I went looking for everyone else. I found Bruce talking to one of Casey's friends so I decided to tell him the plan.

"Hey look, the girls are going to follow you back to the room," I told Bruce real slow so he wouldn't make a scene when he finally realized what I said.

"Oh . . . . Ok. When?"

"I'm going to leave now with Big Boi. Start getting everyone together and leave in about ten minutes. Give me a little time to set up."

"Ok." Bruce said.

"A man, don't mess this up." I had to let him know.

"That's a bet. I got it," Bruce said as we went separate ways. He didn't mind doing the task because he saw that all her friends were drinking.

I told them that I had to go get some gas. I dipped out through the back of the club and headed straight to the truck. When I got to the truck my seats were still reclined and the wrapper was stuck between the seat and the headrest. I took the backstreets going back to the room because I knew the Cops would be out on frontstreet. I already had too many encounters with them.

Campus was dead because everyone was either off-campus partying or passed out. There were only a couple of people walking around campus on Panhellenic Road. I ran up to the room. I started cleaning up as soon as I hit the door. The Player's Palace was not ready for anyone but the player himself. I began throwing everything in the closet, under my bed, under Shawty's bed, and spraying lots of air freshener. All the essentials needed to get those girls draws heavy. I mean, you show a girl that you care just a little bit and those draws get so heavy they hit the ground as soon as they enter the room.

My room was looking nice. It was not the biggest room in college history, but it was nice. I had the black lights in the corners that set the mood. A strobe light for if it ever had a disco party. Then I had a banging play list for whatever nationality I was hosting that night.

There was Jamaican music, Down South music, Up North music, West Coast music, and even a little Arab music for the overseas students. I had one of my Indian boys from down the hall help me out with that one.

As I was picking up the last of the trash I felt a presence; I had the feeling someone was watching me. Looking through my legs while I was bent over, who did I see? Amber. She was standing in my door with some tights, a loose sweat top, and some boots with the fur. Still looking fine, but that is not what we are talking about right now.

She had that look on her face as if she had just heard something. Her eyes were looking at my chest and feet, not looking at my eyes or at my waist. Staying away from these areas will keep her from crying.

"What's wrong?" I said as she just stood there saying nothing, shaking her head.

Wait a minute. "WHAT IS GOING ON?" This isn't normal. What is she doing in my room at this time of the night? Let me go ahead and ask the most important question of the night.

"What are you doing here? What's wrong? There was still no response. "I was on my way over there," I said.

Then I got the most outlandish answer that she could come up with. I mean anything else may have convinced me just by the way she was looking, but her answer was this.

"Nothing. I was just walking around campus," she said under her breath with her head still down.

"FOR WHAT?!?" That was the only thing that I could think of at the time. It may have come out wrong at the time but I'm sorry. She should have come up with a better reason. She must think that I'm stupid or something?

This is the girl that does not go to the club often, if at all. She never stays up past one clock unless she is waiting up for me. Now, out of the blue, she is going to tell me that she was just walking around campus at what was now 3:28 in the morning. I'm not buying it.

Outkast made it perfectly clear that everyone must call before they come; you don't just show up out the blue. That is the rule. What if I wasn't there? She would have felt crazy for walking all the way across campus like that.

I was still new to college, but this lesson never changed from school to school. This was my Caught Up Theory for both males and females if you feel that a person in a relationship with you is sneaking around. First realize where you are; if you are still in school you will be fine. A school, college, or university is the perfect institution for catching a person in a situation. Use a rumor. Rumors spread quickly and can make a person sweat as soon as they hear it. Only a true player can hear a rumor about himself and play the game raw.

"Playing the game raw" is the expression that we use when you really don't care about what is going on with everyone else. You are still going to do your thing. If you act like everything is ok the other person is liable to stick you. Don't forget that males talk just as much as females. I had to remember before engaging in this conversation. The truth might come out. I had to make sure that every word was right and made sense.

I started by asking the questions. This was to get her mind off the subject for a minute. This gave me time to get my story together and prepared to answer any question right away. I couldn't beat around the bush with anything. Looking at Amber, I could tell that she had something to say.

There were two ways that I could have gotten it out of her! I could try to go for the kiss and see if she wanted to talk after she was feeling good, or I could just ask her what she heard and get it over with. Since I was still on my down time from the previous activity that happened hours ago, I decided to ask the question.

"So, what is the REAL reason you are here?" I said realizing that time wasn't on my side.

"Who did you tell not to go to the club?" she said under her breath.

"What are you talking about?" I said like I did not know what was going on.

"You told someone not to go to the club tonight because you were going to be with some other girl."

Knowing where this was going I said, "Who told you this?"

"Does it matter?" Amber said as she looked up with a tear in her eye.

"Yeah, it does if they put my name in their mouth."

"Well, Jamie told me that Bruce . . ."

"Bruce," I said lashing back at her.

"Bruce said that you . . ."

"BRUCE," I proclaimed once again knowing that I shouldn't have trusted that guy.

"She said that you had some girl."

"BRUCE." I kept saying, getting angrier after every time I would say his name.

"And that you had some girls you needed him to make sure that I did not find out about," she finished saying.

"BRUCE," I said for a final time.

"Yeah Bruce. So did you or not?" she finally said with a little ghetto in her voice.

Remember when I told ya'll about haters and how you should never have them in your presence? Well, why didn't I listen to my own advice? I was really getting tired of Bruce getting me jammed up. We had bad vibes since the summer and this was the last time.

Now this lame is going to do something like this. Forget him. If I was not in my right mind I would've left Amber right where she was and went to find him, but I had to deal with this problem first.

I started to pace back and forth between the open door way and then left for about a minute to gather myself. After I walked out of the room, I quickly re-entered just in time as Amber was trying to explain Jamie's story. Jamie was listening from the other room to our conversation.

Jamie was Bruce's girlfriend and my nemesis. She didn't like me or like for Bruce to be around me either. I didn't want to say anything at the time. I had to make sure that I wouldn't say something I would have to apologize for later.

Then she said that one thing that I don't believe should have ever come out of her mouth. "You're worthless." Now ya'll know that I don't believe that males are worthless so I snapped.

"You can get out of my face with all that." I couldn't take it anymore. "I mean you come in here accusing me of doing something that I ain't done. Then you claim that Jamie told you something she heard Bruce say over the phone." Assumption without proof will get you cursed out every time.

"You should know better than to come at me with something like that," I continued. "You know that I don't mess with Bruce like that. So you need to make a decision, either believe me or believe her. Don't let your conscience be the third party in the conversation. You better get your mind right."

I didn't mean to talk to her like that, but I couldn't control myself. Telling me that I was worthless is almost like calling a female a dog. It is a trigger word for me to snap. Her head dropped as those harsh words pierced her heart. I didn't realize how severe the situation was until she lifted her head and the front of her shirt was wet from her tears. I began to feel a little sorrow and wanted her to feel better. That was my goal anyway. "Look at me." I didn't want her to cry.

I had to flip the script; the heat was on so I had to play the victim role. I had to become a victim of the situation in order to make her feel as if it was not of my doing. So I allowed her to tell me what had happened, and I played along and explained where the confusion took place. She had to watch the tone in her voice and stop yelling.

Amber must not have realized that I was constantly leaving the room. Every time I would re-enter she would still be talking. I got the basis of the story, and that was all I needed. Jamie must have heard my voice through the phone. Jamie apparently told Amber that Bruce said I told him, "They can't come to the club."

I even think that Bruce may have had me on a speaker phone. There is no telling with a lame like that. That must have been when Jamie decided to ask Bruce what the two of us were talking about. Now the key to this conversation is that the words "girls", "club", and "don't come" were used all in conjunction with my name. How stupid could he be?

Code Red

"Oh, I forgot that they were on their way up to my room," I thought.

Since it seemed as if I had this end of the situation cleared up, I started working on my Plan B. This was a Code Red Alert. The Code Red Alert was the highest alert in dorm history. This alert went out to all roommates, dorm mates, hallmates, RAs, and potential visitors. Code Red meant that someone has their old lady or main girlfriend in the room and not to bring any random girls or potential relationships to the premises: especially if the random girls are going to the room that's off limits.

I grabbed my phone and threw it in my pocket really quick making sure that Amber didn't see me. Then I went out into the hall. I said I had to go to the bathroom, but I know that she didn't believe that. I went through my phone quick as hell looking for Bruce's number. As I grew closer to the bathroom, I began to hear Bruce's ring tone.

'Walk It Out' was all I could hear from all the way down the hall. Bruce got all the new ringers on his phone, and he likes to let the song play all the way to completion before he picks up the phone. Pick up the phone.

Bruce wasn't answering the phone, trying to be cool with his new ring tones. I had to get Amber out of the room quick. I believe that everyone will have a moment in their lives when their heart starts beating fast and they begin to think with their heart and not their brain. They start saying stupid things and confessing all of their deepest secrets. Well this was not one of those moments for me. I started to think logically.

I grabbed her hand gently, not giving the impression that anything was about to happen. I guided her out the door and to the opposite stairwell in which Bruce and the crew was coming up. "Walk with me." I tried to walk fast but not too fast to the point where she would suspect anything. I could hear their voices growing louder as we reached the end to the hallway. I was hoping that Amber would not be able to recognize any of the voices. I could only hope that Amber wouldn't ask any questions or turn around because I knew that there was no end to Bruce's madness.

The stairwell was warm because the heat was on in the dorms. The walls were covered with graffiti from art work done by the student body. Amber was confused and wanted answers; I could tell by the way she turned around after only going down about three stairs.

"What is wron . . . . ," and I laid one on her. She tried to turn around and start cursing but I met her lips with mine as soon as she opened her mouth.

If there was an award given, I think that I would receive an award for the power of my lips. I made all the words and thoughts disappear from Amber's tongue and mind. Not to brag, but I have made a girl cum just by kissing her softly on her neck once upon a time back in my younger days. The poor female had blacked out and needed smelling salt in order to come to. Amber and I were both very passionate and with both of my hands on each side of her face our souls started to dance. We had been dating for what was almost four months now, and I still had this effect on her. I was good. She was my main concern right now.

"Listen, why are we arguing?" I asked as I held her in my arms. "Jamie and Bruce, come on now. We are better than that to let Jamie and Bruce tear us apart."

"So . . . ," she started to say.

"So, nothing. This is me. Me and you. We are together. Forget about. I'm here with you. Right now."

I sat on the stairs and pulled Amber onto my lap. She wrapped her arms around my neck and laid her head on my shoulders. This was the first time that we had just sat down and really looked at each other. I knew we had a lot in common on the surface, but the depth of a relationship tells how long it will last.

She placed her hand on her chest and held the chain I had given her. "You need me to get your necklace cleaned?" I asked to break the slience.

"If you like," we paused for another long moment. Our foreheads were pressed against each other. Our eyes closed as if we had telepathic communication. We both spoke at the same time then we both paused to let the other talk.

We were both educated so we did have an intelligent conversation. We talked about things that were important to both of us. We discussed things about our future and how we planned to live our lives: issues like abortions. What would happen if she were to get pregnant? She even said that she was for abortion and didn't want to put her life on hold for a child. She wanted to wait until she was out of law school.

I didn't even know her major. She wanted to go to law school. I didn't know. We talked about our old high school, bands, football teams, basketball teams and all types of things that people laugh about for hours. There were so many things that we did not know about each other. Our deepest secrets and fears were placed on the table for openness.

The conversation continued to get deeper. My fear was that I was scared of the dark. Amber stated that she knew, since I slept with my television on.

Then she told me something that changed my life. I knew everything was coming to the surface when I took another look and saw tears coming down her face.

"Someone tried to rape me when I was ten years old."

"Someone? You don't know who?" I said concerned for real at this point.

"I was on my way home. I shouldn't have been out that late, but I wasn't thinking." She stopped talking and I knew why. I didn't ask any more questions. I knew what she was trying to tell me. She eventually came around to telling me that she was walking down the street and a bum tried to rape her in an alley. That is why she valued our relationship the way she did.

Her father left her and her mother when she was little, and then she was almost raped. I was the only man in her life, and she did not want to lose me. I really did not know what to do at this time; a tear was rolling down her cheek and before it could hit the ground I caught it. I told her that everything was going to be all right.

Now came that moment that I was talking about earlier. I broke down. I got caught up in the moment and told her what I had done. I even said that I had done dirt in the past, but would throw it all away for her. I did not cry or anything like that; I just said what was on my mind. I felt it this time.

I did not commit suicide by telling her about all the girls in my life. I just told her that all of my heart was into our relationship, and I was going to change. This was for real, and we held each other for about thirty minutes after our conversation, to the point where we were falling asleep in the stairwell.

And then she said, "I love you."

Yes, that phrase was spoken in my presence, and it kind of felt good and felt real. Someone really loved me and was not just saying it in the heat of a passionate exhibition of baby making. Looking for love was never a top priority, but I guess that it found me in one of my deepest moments. My heart started to beat fast and for some reason my left arm started to tweak.

Some guy named Robert Strenberg said that love involves three components; Intimacy, passion, and commitment. We were intimate and very passionate about each other. The question was with my commitment.

I thought for a second that I was having a heart attack or something. But then it came.

"I love you too."

I said it. I actually said it and for the first time I think I meant it. I know that I meant it. There were certain words that I just didn't say but she found the key to love. I felt like I added "LOVE" to my vocabulary.

This had to be the moment where I became completely caught up and lost most of my swag because I didn't care at this moment. I was committed to her at this time.

The way that I see it is that every person has a relationship with every person that they come in contact with. Once again, how serious your relationship grows is what most people consider. I felt that we had reached another degree of being more serious.

At this point, I felt like my life was changing and for the good. I had a fine girl that really loved me, my energy level was back up, and I was ready for some more baby making exercises. Love making. We had a couple hours before the sun was going to come up. This left just enough time for some of that freaky stuff that you can only do in the dark. We started kissing and caressing each other until the point where we were lost within each other. Then I said jokingly, "Let me get one pump," in a soft whisper.

"I heard that one before," she said laughing at my comment.

"Well let me get two pumps," I said trying to be funny. She had this little school girl look on her face and keep pulling me closer and then turning her head away playing that game.

"Amber, let's go to your room," I said with that look, and she knew what time it was.

"OK," she said in this innocent school girl voice she uses sometimes that she knows I can't resist.

We started walking down the stairwell to the ground floor when Amber jumped on my back. She began to slide down my back after each step that we went down. I grabbed her backside to keep her from falling. She was kissing on my neck as we reached the lobby, and I put her down.

"My turn," I said as I tried to jump on her back.

She kept moving around yelling that I was too big and eventually we ended up going out the door still playing around. And WHAM!!!

What is He doing?

"What are they still doing here?" I said under my breath as we approached the now silent group of people. I mean, it was at least 5:30 by now, and they are still outside the dorm. They stayed thirty minutes away, so I knew by now that they weren't going anywhere any time soon. The half of second that I paused was the half of second that I messed up. Amber could sense the mood change, and my posture probably confirmed the rest of information that she already assumed.

"Nice to see you again," Casey said. "Where did you run off to?"

Bruce was standing right next to Casey with two guys that were a part of some social group on campus Bruce was trying to be a part of.

"Your friend Bruce was kind enough to keep us company." The tension grew in the air as everyone looked at each other. The pieces of the puzzle had fallen into place for Amber and there was nothing that I could say. The two stood there looking at each other up and down.

How can I get out of this situation? I'm stuck here, my girl on one side and my new fling on the other. To top it off, Bruce is looking at me trying to see if I was real enough to play the game.

Then Casey looked at me and said, "Well, where did you go and where did you find this dog?"

Amber looked at me. "Well are you going to answer the question?" Casey added as I looked up at the sky.

"Who is your dog?" Casey asked again directing her question at Amber.

WHAM!!!

I really couldn't believe what happened next. The sudden attack was so quick that no one around was prepared. Oh no. It was not me getting knocked out. Casey's head hitting the ground was payback enough for Amber. Calling Amber a dog was not smart.

It was like Mike Tyson fighting one of those white boys and knocking them out in the first round. I was kind of proud that my girl could fight. I guess that the word "dog" just has that certain effect on some females that makes them snap.

"Yeah baby, now that's what I am talking about. Don't let no one talk to you like that," I said proudly thinking that the situation was over.

I felt that our talk was enough to get me through without saying nothing. Just to stand by her was going to be good.

"Get out of my face and leave me alone," Amber said turning around with tears coming down her face.

"I don't ever want to talk to you again. You lied to me. You was with this girl tonight. I trusted you with my heart, and this is how you treated me. Trust. Trust hell." She was screaming uncontrolla-bly. Her soul was crying out at this time. Everything that was bot-tled up was being released right in my face. It felt like an emotional water hydrant was hitting my heart. I had never felt that type of emotion come from a female.

This was love. I was losing her love with every word that was coming out of her mouth. Every syllable felt like needles. Anger and hate were pouring out.

What could I say? My words meant nothing at this moment. I could have sworn on my mother's life, and she still wouldn't have believed a word.

"You're a bastard, as long as you think with your private and not your heart." There was a long pause in her voice. "My heart will never be able to beat on the same pace as yours," Amber said with a calm tone as she turned toward her room and started to walk away leaving me with nothing but the desire of wanting to be with her.

"Amber . . . Amber . . . . Amber," I called her name three times. I even thought of going after her. As I took the first step, Casey decided to get up and start yelling before Amber could get out of hearing range.

"You better run! You think this is over." I immediately turned around to confront Casey.

Her hair was messed up and her make-up was running down the side of her face. I wanted to laugh and call her stupid, but I just stood there with a smirk on my face.

"You are so stupid. You really don't remember me, do you?"

I began to look harder at her now since her glasses were broken and her face began to change now since the sun was starting to rise. Her make-up was starting to fade.

"Your name isn't Lo. I know your real name," she said as if she'd discovered the cure for melanoma.

The way she said my name I knew she had to know me, and I had done something terrible to her. This was the first time that I saw her without her sunglasses on, and she looked completely different.

"You made me kill our baby, and you don't know who I am," she said trying to be loud enough for everyone to hear. "The last time I saw you was when you were walking me out of the abortion clinic."

I remembered her. This was the daughter of the freaky mother. She really grew up in two years, but forget all that. This girl was crazy showing up like this. Now I remember her. She tried to pull that same virgin thing with me the first time I hit.

This female might be bipolar. I wrote the check and got rid of that child as quick as she told me she was pregnant. Plus, I was leaving to go to college so I wasn't studying her. Her middle name was Casey, but her first name was Lauren. She had to be crazy coming up here with all this mess. How did she find me?

"Just answer me. Why?" Casey said looking for an explanation.

"Why what?" I replied shocked that she didn't know the answer.

"Why haven't I seen or heard from you since that day." I had to stop this madness right here because she was starting to really piss me off.

"You really thought I was going to let you have my kid? How stupid could you be? You wasn't about to mess up my dream. It was one night. Get over it. We had fun. That was it."

"That's all it was to you?" she asked looking around to see if anyone was listening to what I was saying.

"You really thought that you lucked up and caught one. Well, I ain't the one." I got serious to the point where my intentions started to show on my face. Anger was coming out of my pores, and my skin was tightening.

I began to walk towards her so she could hear me very clearly. I didn't want to raise my voice but the look on my face let everyone (even those lame social group boys) that I was not playing.

"Listen to me very closely because I will not repeat myself. Look at you. You are nothing to me. You came all this way to prove what? Nothing. Nothing you can do will affect me. You really thought that I liked you. It was just one night. Get over it." I started to walk away, and she grabbed my arm.

"I'll slap the mess out of you if you ever touch me again," I cocked back and raised my hand. Then Bruce decided to open his mouth.

"Come on, shawty. You ain't got to talk to her like that," Bruce said, sounding concerned.

"Did you raise your hand so I could call on you? No. So don't ever speak out of line. Who are you to try and tell me what to do? You're a female just like her . . . so you can shut up talking to me too."

I thought I was going to have to hit him because he began to walk over to me, but he extended his hand and said, "Shawty, I'm on your side."

I looked at Bruce and shook my head. "You just don't get it, do you?" I walked away from everyone. I had to think for a minute. If I would have stayed I would have been arrested for murder: not attempted murder but murder.

Final Thoughts: "The streets are called the concert jungle because humans take on animal characteristics in order to survive. As the day meets night the mentality of the corrupt becomes the ideal of the just, and human nature finds greed, envy, and lust in every corner that it looks."

Chapter VII

NOW WHAT

*"The true test of the seventh letter is not what he does or knows, but more so
if he keeps learning in order to grow."*

I Don't Know

I DON'T know what happened after I left the parking lot. I went
back up to my room, and locked the door behind me. I messsed
up. It was Saturday morning, and the sun was starting to shine
through my dorm room curtains. This crazy girl Casey had just
ruined my perfect life. As I got up to close the curtains, I could see
Bruce was still standing there looking silly as if he had nothing to
do with the entire situation.

I allowed one dumb boy to take over my pyramid. I felt hope-
less. I loved Amber, and I knew that she was the girl that I wanted
in my life. Didn't I? I mean I did tell her that, and I know that I
meant it. I could really feel something different.

I had to think where I went wrong. Love is an emotion. The
problem is that I forgot that women are very emotional creatures.
I said I loved her before I cancelled out the lust. I was in love with
Amber but lusted for Casey or something confusing like that.

We, as males, tend to treat females as if they have male characteristics. Whenever a man tells a woman that he loves her, he then
has a lot of responsibility on his hands. What it really comes down

to, is that most men feel as if they deserve the best in life; the finest car, biggest house, finest wife.

Sometimes we know that we can't have the finest female in the world because we might not be the most attractive male, but a man will search and search until he finds that one fine girl that is for him. This is a message for all of my males as well as females. There is a point system which we as materialistic humans have invented.

I introduced my notion of cute and ugly people, and the point system in which they should live by earlier. The simple fact is that people usually accept the way they look in the mirror. So, when they see a person with similar characteristic as themselves, they become comfortable in a relationship with that person. In this point system, there is a one point radius in which a person can go outside of their own point. A four in the point system should be with another four, an eight with an eight, and so on and so forth.

Yes. It is true that every person has someone special, but let's just start being real with ourselves. When a man puts all of his heart into a relationship with a female, that is when he places his dreams on the table also. I was ready to include Amber into my dreams and vice versa with hers. I had to make this right.

Females don't see it, but men cry. Not in front of everybody, so not to make a scene like ya'll females do, but we cry. I knew a guy that was going with his girl for four years, four years now, and the girl got married to another guy four months after they broke up. He cried.

I didn't fall asleep until about two hours later. I woke up in a cold sweat. That scared me. I had a dream I was walking alone through a party and no one knew who I was. I guess my deepest fear was being alone, but I never knew it because I was never alone. I had been physically alone many times, but this mental loneliness was killing me. I turned on the TV to get my mind off of the subject. I had to do a lot of stuff but I didn't feel like moving at all.

My study group was meeting this morning. Saturdays at ten o'clock was our scheduled time, but I was in no rush to get up and go. I was going to catch up on my sleep and get up in time to go lift weights at about two. I laid my head down and started to doze off when I heard someone knocking.

I wasn't going to get up. Knock knock. Keith and Shawty walked in the room. They were laughing so I knew they had heard what had happened. I could have sworn that I locked the door. I think one of them got my key.

"What are ya'll doing up. Don't neither one of ya'll have anything better to do on Saturday. Do ya'll ever sleep?" I said thinking to myself that they need to get out.

"We were just leaving from these girls' room on campus and decided to see how you were doing." Shawty said smiling.

"So, get up and don't act like that. You know what we want. Tell the truth. Did Amber knock Casey out?" Keith said laughing out loud.

I knew that was all that they wanted. "Yeah, man. I can't even look at Casey the same anymore. At first she was cute, but now she could be the newest member of the Black Eyed Peas," Keith said jokingly but with a straight face.

"I'm hungry," Shawty said looking into the refrigerator.

"You cut, right?" That was Keith's way to ask if we had relations. "Cause her friends weren't talking about anything. They all had boyfriends."

"Well you know how I do." My swag wasn't gone I just had to redirect my focus.

I had to tell the story of who Casey really was. I started by telling them what happened in the truck, the room, and in the parking lot. They laughed the entire time, and it was even kind of funny as I was telling it.

"Ahh, the little baby is all alone and wants his diaper. All of the ladies in his life are gone. Well everything will be back to normal this weekend," Shawty said as they left the room.

"What's going on this weekend?" I asked as I jumped up and ran to the door just to ask that important question.

"The Hellenic Ball. Duh," Keith replied as the elevator door closed.

I forgot all about the Hellenic Ball. Now what? I can't get Amber back, and I don't want to ever see Casey again. I will look like the biggest fool if I go by myself.

By Myself

Those fools finally left my room, and I was able to get an hour of sleep before my Saturday started. On top of practice, I had a lot of other things to worry about. Oh, ya'll think that I forgot about Bruce. I don't think so. He was on my hit list, and we had to lift weights at the same time today. I wasn't planning on approaching him, but I was ready for whatever was going to happen.

I didn't even bother going by the café because I knew that everybody would be in there talking about what happened last night. I figured that my only reason for going in there would be to see Amber, but I did not want to cause a scene. Nothing is more embarrassing then having your girl not wanting to talk to you in public. You end up looking like the begging member in the relationship.

It's like girls always want to have conversations, but when they are around other girls they let them speak for them. That is so weird to me.

I went and got some lunch from an off campus spot and ate in the locker room. What most people think about a traditional locker room, being dirty and nasty, is completely opposite from ours. We had a couple of lounge chairs, big screen TVs, and a pool table where I won everyone's weekend money.

Keith walked in and sat next to me. "Can I ask you something?"

"What's happenin'," I replied.

He sat there for a minute as he gathered his thoughts. His face started to change. He started to stutter then he blurted out "Man, my girl is trying to take my child away from me." He leaned back in the lounge chair and took a deep sigh and then continued.

"She talking about going back home and taking the child with her." He looked mad, but I didn't have anything to say. I didn't have any kids so I never knew how it felt to have one taken.

"So what are you going to do?" That was the only question I could think of asking.

"I'm going to talk to coach now. I'm going to finish this season, but I don't know about next year. I might have to transfer back home." He had a confused look on his face and I was in a situation where I knew nothing to say. The whole situation with the baby was strange all together because the time line of the months don't add up. He insisted that the child was his though I didn't want to bring that subject up again or he would have been really mad then. I needed him to focus on one thing at a time.

"I know that things aren't going right, right now. But I know one thing. Don't go to coach until you figure out exactly what you are going to do," I told him.

"Why?" he looked back at me and said.

"Why? You don't remember? Why Steve ain't here no more?" Steve was a junior that got mad at the coach and decided to transfer. Instead of getting everything ready to transfer first, Steve told the coach about his plans. Steve was black-balled from every University that our head coach had connections with.

"Steve was different. That guy was crazy!" Keith exclaimed.

"Still don't tell coach until you find out what is really going to happen. You never know what coach is thinking."

"I feel ya," he said as he got up and touched his toes. "I have to go get some ice from the training room. You need something?

"Forget Sam. He tried to get me in trouble." Sam was our head trainer and really didn't like me because I never came to get rehab.

"Matter of fact, tell Sam to kiss my butt when you go in there."

"Whatever. Sam been working out on the low." We were both laughing as he headed out the door.

I had to get my big homie back felling good. I didn't like to see him worrying about his child, or whoever's child. That's my last time joking about that. I would try my best to get off the subject and get him focused back on football. By this time, everyone began to walk in the locker room about one-thirty with different versions of what had happened last night.

"Hey, I heard you got locked up last night," one senior offensive lineman asked when he walked in.

"Yeah, and your mother did my cavity search." He just wanted to say something. "Next time, tell her to at least buy me a drink before she starts feeling on me," I think he was trying to be funny, but I wasn't laughing. Where do people get these stories from?

As Bruce walked in, I kept my cool and played the whole situation sideways. I was not going to let a lame affect my day. I did the same thing that I usually did. I sat around chilling watching the TV that was in front of my locker.

"Have a nice night?" Bruce asked under his breath as he walked by my locker.

"Oh, so you think that you are a comedian, huh?" I said to calm his actions down.

"Well, Casey sure thought that I was very entertaining," Bruce said giving another player a high five.

"What did you say? Ain't nothing changed from last night," I said to let him know that I was not in a playing mood.

He was making jokes, but wasn't nothing funny. My patience was growing thin. The fact he was bragging about a female that he didn't even hit made him look real lame.

"Whatever. We all know what time it is," he said under his breath.

"What time is it then?" I said as I got up out of my locker.

"What are you getting up for? Can't take a joke?" Bruce said trying to bring attention to the area.

"Ain't nothin' funny," I said getting closer and purposely invading his comfort zone. I wanted him to do something to set me off.

"Boy, you better get out of my face," he said quickly and full of neverous energy.

"Or what?" I answered. "What you going to do if don't?" At this point, he had to do something because everyone was starting to take interest in what was taking place. I could see him balling up his fist as if he was getting mad or something.

"Don't make that mistake and try to get gangsta' cause I promise I won't miss," I said just loud enough for him to hear.

I was tired of looking at him. I said let's ride. I was in a lose-lose situation and the only way out was to set the tone. I swung and knocked him out. I was about twenty pounds heavier but that did not matter. I was from the streets and knew how to fight. I may have lost the battle, but I was not going to lose the war.

I connected with the first punch across his jaw. After I saw his reaction, I went after him again and the second one went straight across his eye. About five people had to hold me back. His nose started to run and it was obvious that he was not expecting me to react like that. I was cursing and trying to break free from my teammates.

In the heat of the moment, Keith walked back into the locker room and saw what was going on. He knew that I had jumped on Bruce and immediately grabbed me and took me into the shower area to calm down. He was trying to make sure that I would not get into any more trouble.

"It aint worth it," he kept saying trying to calm me down.

"I'm straight," I kept repeating to convince myself. I was still ready. If Keith would have let me go, I would've went after him again.

"I'm not letting you go," Keith said as we stood there looking in the mirror.

"Shawty look . . . look shawty. Don't do this here. Wait." Keith was serious so I began to listen.

As we were looking in the mirror I could see that the talk we had earlier was affecting him. He was trying to help me like I had helped him. He was trying to talk to me.

One of the assistant coaches walked in.

"Coach wants you in his office." Then he looked at me again. "Now," he said letting me know that it was serious.

I took another minute to wash my face and think. I messed up and knew it. I headed up stairs and the door to the coaches' office was open.

"You already got your invitation. What are you waiting on?" Coach said as I stood in the doorway.

"What are we going to do with you? You are almost making it a point to stay in trouble. It's almost out of my hands. This is the first week of school and this is your second fight in the locker room. There was no telling how many altercations you have had on the field," Coach looked mad, but he was still calm.

"Coach, this time it wasn't me"

"That's what you say every time. It's never you."

"But coach . . ."

"I don't want to hear it. I'm going to give you one more time, and then changes are going to be made. We can't have this type of off field activity in our program." He paused then looked me in my eyes.

"What's going on? This is your chance to talk to me. Tell me something." He wanted me to tell him everything just so he could have something to talk about, but he wasn't my life coach; he was my football coach. I wasn't saying nothing to him in which he could judge my on-field performance. Anyone who has ever been to jail knows not to tell the people that have control over your situation what is really going on. They go from control over a certain aspect to control over your entire life. It's social talk as well as personal talk.

"It's nothing. What's my punishment?" I was ready to leave. This was between me and Bruce. It had nothing to do with coach.

"The next time you get into any type of little trouble, and it gets back to me, I'm going to place you on probation. Is that understood?"

"Yeah."

"Since you want a punishment, see Coach Speed, and he will give you all the punishment you need." Coach Speed was our strength coach and usually handed out disciplinary actions.

Well, Bruce did have to explain his black eye. He could have said anything besides the fact that I attacked him. I knew he was going to tell because he didn't live by any code of honor. His father wasn't around when he was growing up so he developed his speak pattern from his mother. He would often smack his lips and roll his eyes when he would get mad.

I learned from being in jail a couple of days for a DUI. Whatever happens, happens, but you never tell because the consequences of telling are greater. Plus, you lose all respect. Bruce sounded like a female as we both sat in the coach's office.

"He just went off and hit me, Coach," Bruce told the receiver coach. I should have beat him up in front of our coach so they could have seen how much of a female he really was.

By the time we finished talking to the coach, Bruce had wiggled his way out of trouble and I found myself running hills after my lift was over. It was nothing. I knew how good it felt when I punched Bruce in his face. That more than made up for the punishment.

Since no one was around when I was running, I began to think and laugh about the situation. It had really gotten out of hand, and I had to find a way to bring things back together.

Tomorrow was Sunday and the beginning of a new week. The weekend was over, and I spent the remainder of my Saturday night in my room by myself. I didn't feel like going anywhere. I decided to let everything blow over before I hit the streets again. I found an alternate plan for going out, resorting to my pyramid.

This is where the base did the most good, so I called a chick. I meant to say "well-qualified female" for assistance. Confidence is always needed in these critical situations. What better girl than this one girl named Liz who was a proven pro at what she did?

I would usually call Liz about once a month just to learn all of the new tricks. Liz was a stripper and was real good working the pole. She was a little older than me and often wanted to teach me new things to use on my girls. She was good at doing her job.

"You on deck for tonight?" Was usually the only question that I would ask Liz when I called her.

"Yeah."

"Call before you come," is how I would end the conversation. It was cool having a relationship like this one because neither one of us expected to take any additional step to pursue a more meaningful relationship. We were open with our relationship and acted as first time lovers each time we were together.

Back to Dating

I must have slept for about thirteen hours because I didn't wake up until about four o'clock Sunday afternoon. As I lay in the bed watching Sports Center, I realized that I had even a bigger problem on my hands, The Hellenic Ball was coming up this weekend.

I went to my black book for help. I called my first attendant. Her name was Kristina. Kristina and I met at an academic conference in high school. She was rich. Her father was worth over twenty—five million dollars.

"What are you doing this weekend, baby? You need to come see me," I asked Kristina.

"I have to fly out to Cali this weekend with my parents. They are sponsoring this hair show. I'm sorry," she replied.

Well, that's why I have a second attendant. Ashley wasn't rich at all but smarter than a little bit. She never went out or went to the club. Ashley was probably the world's best keep secret. This girl was fine.

"You haven't called me in three days," I said as she answered the phone.

"I know. I have been so busy working on this project."

"Well, tell me that you have time to go to the ball with me this weekend?"

"I would love to, but . . ." she said

"But what?" I replied, trying to change her mind even before I heard her reason.

"You forgot about our last conversation?"

"I don't think so." I was trying to remember if it was her birthday or not.

"I told you last week I was going to be a mentor at the FCA camp Friday and Saturday."

"Oh yeah. I thought you were talking about something else." I completely forgot.

"I thought you were going to go with me?" She started asking me.

"I was . . . hold on," I clicked over and just sat the phone down. I had to think of a good reason to get off the phone.

"Hello"

"Yeah," Ashley answered.

"I'm going to call you right back," I said hanging up before she answered. Ashley was sweet and wasn't tripping. She knew I wasn't going to any Christian Camp with her.

I had come up on a problem, and the only way to get out of it was to start recruiting. I guess it was back to dating. I always keep a reserve list for this type of situation. These females are from a selective group. I probably met them one time somewhere and thought they were cute. I hadn't called them because I was probably just too busy. I could remember that they had potential, and that is what counts in a crucial situation. These females are sometimes even unknown to my closest friends.

From my reserve list I had to pull together the bad-dest females from each of the neighboring schools. They had to be the cream of the crop. This was that girl that every guy on campus wanted to get at but couldn't seem to find out where she was hiding. Well now you know; she's with me. I never felt that I had a lot of females, I just knew that I had the females that every one else wanted.

Remember that in order to be a member of the reserve list, please, I mean please, don't let me hit on the first night. Then you will drop to the base of the pyramid with the dogs and cows.

These females are solely reserves and replacements for the royal court. I can't have a freak as a representative of me. My main girl cannot have a track record of being around the block. That might sound a little harsh, but what in life isn't?

So Monday rolls around, and I decided to call Carmen. I met Carmen about a month ago standing outside a club. She was being rushed at the time by her friends, but I could tell she was about something. Carmen was bad, looked almost Dominican, but she claims that her father was black. I didn't really know what to expect and wasn't about to spend a lot of money. I went straight to my hook-up spot, Rancho Mexican Restaurant. It was expensive, but I knew the host and she would always look out.

I drove ten minutes to pick her up so we could go out. I didn't realize she was still in high school until I heard her say, "What time are you going to have me back?"

"How old are you?" I slowed the car up to ask just in case I had to turn around if she was too young. I had a policy about age. A female must be half a man's age plus seven. Since I was nineteen, she had to be at least seventeen.

"I'm eighteen. I turned eighteen last month," she said looking like she was ready to have fun now that she was old enough.

"Just checking," I replied as we rode off.

She was fine, don't get me wrong, but I didn't know she was a slacker. Slackers might be the worse type of people to be around because they are so similar to haters. Slackers are female haters (girls that don't have anything but talk about the girls that do). Haters hate on things they want but don't have. Slackers just hate and don't want to have. It's kind of weird to explain. Trust me, when you meet a slacker, you will know.

For example, we were sitting at the dinner table and an attractive female walked by. I knew she was still in high school but that doesn't excuse her mentality. The other girl in my eyes was very attractive and could dress, but here comes Carmen.

"That Bebe doesn't look right on her, and those boots are just too high. She must be a stripper," Carmen said as the young lady walked by.

I looked under the table to let Carmen know I was looking at her shoes. You have on Reebok, and you're cool with it. Reeboks are never cool so instead of hating, she needed to be participating. I would be crazy if I paid to take a girl out that didn't know how to dress for the occasion.

The whole night was a mess. Her only purpose was to say that she was out with a college guy. I couldn't take this girl to the Hellenic Ball or anywhere else for that case. I had a couple of drinks to knock the edge off, but after awhile I was ready to go.

She was lame and looked like she would cause a scene in public. The fact that she had a tattoo on her lower back did not turn me on anymore. The cute little flower was starting to look more like a plant. I still took her back to the room after dinner. I had to get back what I paid for.

There was no excitement or rush in our relationship. I was really just using her to get a rush and get a good night-sleep. I didn't have the feeling of getting caught up to keep the passion going. Since it was late she felt like she could spend the night. That was a no-no. I kicked her out right after I was finished. Once I grabbed my keys she knew what time it was.

Now, Tuesday was a different beast. I went to the movies with this senior from FSU after practice. I chose the movies because I really didn't feel like talking. This was the best place where talking wasn't allowed. For some reason, she forgot that aspect. Her name was Monique, and she was from a small country town outside Chicago. She was a real country girl at heart who was just getting introduced to technology.

"This is a big movie theater." It was relatively small, but I let her think what she wanted.

She was fascinated by the big city life and found everything to be the most remarkable thing she had every seen. Modern technology was not her expertise, and I soon found out as the opening credits began.

This turned out to be the movie date from hell. Her phone kept ringing causing everyone to look at us and shake their heads. It had to ring at least three times before the movie even started. It was like she did not know there was a vibrate setting or didn't know how to use it.

"Hey girl . . . I'm at the movies . . . I don't even know . . . what is this movie we watchin'?" I didn't answer.

"Girl, he acting like he don't hear me. He so crazy." She hadn't seen crazy. If she didn't put that phone up she was going to see crazy very soon.

"The movie is starting," I tried to say in a calm manner.

"Ok girl, let me call you back. Yeah girl, the movie is starting." She hung up.

"I'm sorry baby. You mad at me?" Then this country girl had the nerve to have a conversation during the movies. Mid-way though her conversation I snatched the phone from her ear and hung it up. She was shocked, but I didn't care. Moments later I felt something vibrate and thought that she finally got the idea. As it turns out, she had a pager. Are you kidding me? Pagers went out with Cross Colours and Paco-Jean outfits.

To top it all off, she wanted to make-out in the movie theater. Don't nobody do that no mo'. Watch the movie that I paid for, and shut up while you are doing it. I took her straight back to her campus after that episode. There had to be someone in this city that qualified to be seen in public.

Wednesday's date lasted about 15 minutes. She was nothing that I imagined. In fact, I felt like I was tricked. I had to get her friends number, but her friend was getting the number for her. She was a native, so I went to her mother's house to pick her up. There was trash all in the yard. The screen door didn't have a screen. The guard dog sounded like he had bronchitis, and there were two Mexican midgets next door arguing about something.

I pulled up at the house, dialed her number, and bonged the horn. I was not getting out. "Come on out," I said as she answered the phone.

I didn't know who this big girl was that was walking towards my truck. I knew one thang, it wasn't going down like this.

So what did I do? I played the game raw and left her where I found her. I headed straight back to the room and turned off my phone. I had a paper due the next day so I did that and went to sleep.

Dating was much more fun when I had a girlfriend waiting at the end of the night. That way if my date didn't go right, I always had a place to go. Thursday afternoon was my real drop-off point. I had been on three bad dates, and it was not looking so good for the home team. The week was almost over, and I was starting to think about Amber. I was going on my third day without having any relations with anyone and all my boys were getting on me for what happened the week before.

Was it me or had the game changed? The game doesn't change just the players in it.

So I went back and re-evaluated the situation. I just started seeing females in a different way ever since last weekend. I had to pay more attention to how these females were acting and all of the little petty things I would easily have overlooked in the past. The little things did not bother me as much when I had someone else. Even in the midst of defeat, I could not lower my standards just to have someone in my life.

There were two days left to find someone to go to the ball with, and I was not going to call Amber. I hadn't seen her walking around campus and was not sure if she was trying to avoid me. It was as if she changed her whole schedule.

As the night fell, there was no talk about going anywhere so I headed to the athletic complex to print out my paper. This was my first Thursday not going out, and I really didn't feel like going anywhere. I just wanted to be alone. It was just my luck that everybody had the same idea that night.

"Dog, just go and talk to Amber. I mean you obviously love her," Justin said, trying to make a joke as I walked in to the room with my head down.

The computer lab was full of the football team because some teacher was giving a mid-term in the morning, and they had mandatory study hall.

"And why do you say that?" I had to say as I sat down at one of the computers.

"What is today? Thursday right? You are where? My point exactly," he said, trying to bring reality back to the situation.

"Yeah man, I mean what's the big deal? Everyone knows what happened, and everyone knows that you love her. Just go make up. You know you wouldn't be able to handle seeing Amber with another guy," Smiles said with a smile on his face.

"Are you trying to get with my girl?" I said jokingly, acting as if I was getting defensive.

"Calm down shawty. Ain't nobody trying to get with your girl. It's just that you know the Hellenic Ball is in two days, and you know everyone thinks that she is on the market," Smiles said in his Atlanta accent.

"Shawty, I feel you, but she won't even talk to me . . . and I really ain't worried about her," I had to reply.

"If you are the man that I know, it won't take you long to figure out how to get her back," Smiles said trying to give me a little motivation.

So I did call. Soon as I left study hall I called, but she didn't pick up. Five times I called, and she did not pick up once. This was not her room phone but her cell phone. She never leaves her phone anywhere, and I know that she doesn't take thirty minute showers. This could only mean one thing. SHE WAS WITH ANOTHER GUY.

I had to be over exaggerating. She wouldn't jump into another relationship that quick. That would be a slap in my face. That means that I really did not mean anything to her and at any given time could have been replaced. I could not go out like this, so I got desperate. I called my ex.

Let me explain my Being Out with an Ex Theory. If you are in another city, an ex—can be used as a confidence booster. This is cool and very interesting to see how people on campus react to someone new. I call this "waking them up". Now this does not hold true if you are in the same city as your ex. That would just be considered going back and not moving forward, which we don't want.

This is for every man across the world; never, I mean never, be seen in public with your ex unless it is an emergency, but I did it because I was desperate. Jody Dixon was my one-year three month high school sweetheart. She was one of the finest girls that I ever went with. I still keep her picture in my wallet to show people how fine she was. We broke up for obvious reasons. She thought that I was going to cheat on her in college, which I did.

We never really broke up. We just kind of separated from each other. She was not shocked when she found out because she knew that it would happen sooner or later. I remember when I gave her a promise ring. Bad idea. Now every time I see her she asks the same question. "Remember when you gave me this ring for Christmas?" Yeah, and I only bought the ring because it was on sale, and I could not afford anything else. Since I was desperate, I did ask her to go to the Ball with me and she said yes, of course.

It was only Thursday, and Jody still had time to make it since she went to school about three hours away in North Carolina. Jody planned on flying in, but I convinced her to drive her new Lexus hard top convertible that her father gave her for graduating high school. I wanted to drive it. I had everything planned as far as my date, but there were other things that I needed to set up in order to get Amber back. First, I had to make sure that she was going to be there.

For this special mission, I had to get the best in the business. I went straight to Shay and Squeak to find out everything that I needed to know about what was going on in Amber's life. I had to pay them for their service, and I knew the perfect way how. They both needed a man in their lives, and I knew who they liked. I had to beg Sam and Tay to take them out one time, but they owed me a favor anyways. Within two hours, Shay and Squeak gave me a full report.

Apparently, Amber was on the phone with someone in the café and stated that she was going to pick this person up from the airport Saturday morning she said that she had already gotten their tickets to the ball. Shay and Squeak were not really sure who it was. All they knew was that she sounded very excited about his person's arrival. That was all the information that I needed.

Well, since I knew that she was going to be at the ball with someone else, I had to find a way to stunt. I had to hit the mall. I knew this girl that worked at Prime Shop, the best clothing store in the city for urban wear. We had to be in the latest gear, cleanest ride, and I had to get my dreads braided. Last but not least, I had to make sure that Jody was going to be the finest thing at the ball.

Final Thoughts: Cherish life and remember moments and not days. When you remember days, you often forget about some great moments.

(Insert)

A letter to MySelf,

Just shut the f*&k up and listen to what I have to say. Cause this is the same s(%t, you would have said back in the day. Remember when you said, "If you really want me, then b^*#h go digital." Or even some smooth s(%t that you know, she didn't know. What the f^&k you got to flex for? You can really make that p^$@y sore. Fall asleep, she don't want no more. Let the pit lose, and let the lion roar.

So, b^*#h stop playing. Go ahead and change the game. F*&k what a hater say. And lames are basically all the same. Please let Da' King mentality come out and reign, real stories based on the truth about the game. I know you don't talk much, that's why I never said anything about the booth. But believe me, writing that s(%t down and you can be the truth. And I like how you still keep your swag, cause that the real proof. Royalty and loyalty, to my mom and to my dad, man. Purple is my rag man. Man, you don't really want to make me mad, man.

Long armed gorillas in these streets. You know only lions set where we meet. And knowledge from the elders is what we keep. I'm tired of walking when you sleep. Let me go wake up CT, because you know he'll be ready to ride out. Pull up in something stupid, and go straight to the hide out. You aint fooling no one, I listen to the verses and not the hook. B^*#h you think you know me just because you read my book. There's a whole different side of me, just ask Stone and Cook.

So what the f*&k we waiting for? And I'm only going to ask once mo, "What the f*&k we waiting for?" Let me find out that you're doing this s(%t on purpose. And, all that praying that you are doing, aint even going to be worth it. Cause the game is 85% mental, so you better get your mind right. And, I aint letting up on you no mo. That wouldn't sound right. I'm asking nicely for you to let me loose now. Or we can rewind this story over and I'll be Bruce now.

Live for the moment and not the day, because the beginning never tells the ultimate fate. You can't fool me into thinking it's ok, just because You got up today. I know why your eyes stay red with passion. And it has nothing to do with material objects or fashion. You're a real product of the royal blood line. The real royal blood line, where we use our God given ability, f*&k any and every dollar sign. B^*#h, you been holding me back for too long now it's my time. I'm ready to shine.

I'm just telling you this so you won't stop grinding man. Catch this quick come-up to provide for your children's land. It's all in you, like a one-man marching band. But instead of staying up, hanging out, why don't you try chillin out. And really read the cards that the dealer is dealing out. This is my letter to my future. Stand tall when sinners throw stones and always crawl to the throne. And if ever there was a Son of Man then I Am his clone. The second coming has arrived!

Chai'
3891 B.C.

Chapter VIII

STEPPIN OUT

"Even if life has a strange way of playing out, I'm still going to be fly when I'm stepping out."

The Ball

THE day of the ball came around. Jody had arrived early Saturday morning. Her new ride was clean, and I knew that this was going to be a great day and a wonderful night. I had our day already laid out; the reservations for dinner were already made, and everything was in place. I made Jody a hair appointment at one of the top salons in town. I wanted everything to be straight, so even if my plan didn't work I would already have plan B in place. It's sort of like an On-going Plan B.

After Jody finished getting her hair done, we went and relaxed for the rest of the day at a spa. We spent most of the time there catching up on old times. The Day Spa was one of my favorites places to go when I got stressed. They do your feet, hands, and back. It is the most relaxing experience. If you could do it, you would, too.

The night came so fast. It was time to go to the ball before we knew it. The anticipation gave me butterflies in my stomach like I was about to play a football game. This was going to be perfect. Jody was still beautiful.

We finally got back to the room and changed for the Ball. Jody's body was bad. I didn't really have a plan for when I got to the ball; I was just going to wing it. The way Jody was looking I was almost like, "forget the Ball". I touched Jody on the butt, just to see what type of person she had become in college.

"You grab me, and I'm going to grab you back." Yes sir, that was all that I wanted to hear. Nothing had changed between us. No matter how long we were away from each other, once we looked each other in the eyes with seduction, it was over. It only took that one look. It really didn't matter whether it was a minute, a moment, or a month; Jody and I had moved passed love and were loyal to each other.

She was lucky that I put a lot of effort into the night because I was ready to cancel right then. We eventually got dressed after chasing each other around naked for a while. I had to release some of this tension that was in the room. Plus, we were just going to stunt, anyways. No biggie, right?

We pulled up clean with the top dropped. Everyone was still outside waiting to get in. The valet was stupid. Everyone was in big bodies. All eyes turned as we strolled down the walkway. This was a Red Carpet Event, so the walk was the highlight of the night. People were taking pictures, and we were the center of focus. Jody was *puttin on*, and I was the King of the Campus once again. I had bounced back like no other.

"I see ya boi!!" Somebody yelled from a distance. I really couldn't see who it was, but I still threw the deuces back.

Jody and I became the life of the party as soon as we walked in the building. People were everywhere, and it was near impossible to walk around once we got inside. The theme of the party was Ghetto Fly, and everyone was in their freshest gear. All eyes were looking at my new piece of meat. I was laced down in some of the hottest new Swag Purple Label with the hat to match.

The party was crunk, but you know who I was looking for. This whole night meant, nothing if Amber didn't show up. I was stuntin' on everyone, and she had to see me. I had to make my way around the concert hall. The room seemed to get bigger and bigger as I walked through the crowd.

Yes sir, I could see her. Amber. I had to be stupid. Jody didn't have nothing on Amber. She was still beautiful from afar. I had to get over there, but I had to get rid of Jody first.

Knowing me, I eased away from Jody for a couple of minutes and left her on the dance floor with the Crew. I headed towards the bar so she would think I was going to get some drinks. As I got closer, I noticed that Amber was shaking and her hands were covering her face. So, I sped up like *captain saver* or some body.

"Ha-ha-ha." She was not crying, but laughing.

From my view, I did not notice this big headed, jerry curl wearing, turtle and the hare lookin' guy sitting beside her.

"Oh hey. This is Kevin," she said still laughing at whatever this lame was telling her. Then she completely ignored my existence and continued to laugh. She got out of her seat and gave me a church hug. Amber then took a look at her drink that was sitting next to Kevin's arm.

Then get this, she then downs the drink that was in her hand. I was not sure if she was drunk, but I could tell that she had been drinking.

"Kevin, you want to dance?" she said once again ignoring my total existence.

What was that? I have got to be dreaming. He wasn't cuter than me. She had downgraded. There was nothing that I could do. I could either look like a lame and stop them; causing a scene. Confess my love in front of everyone; which wasn't about to happen. Or, I could be a G and tell her later. I knew she was going to be at the Spot after this.

I brought some more drinks and watched everyone having a good time for a couple of songs. This was kind of getting to me. Amber had got swallowed by the number of people on the dance floor. Nothing was going right.

"Here take this," I told Jody as I handed her a drink.

"You OK?" She must have seen something in my face that said I wasn't having a good time.

"I'm good," I had to change my demeanor because I was not going to let this affect the rest of my night.

With the way I was feeling, I sure wasn't about to lose Plan B too. I got her a drink and kept her by me. Plus, I had the keys to her car, so if she did decide to leave I was going to do the same.

"Why won't you dance with me?" Jody said as she raised my arm and snuggled under my shoulder.

"You know I don't dance. I'm a gangsta."

"Oh really," she said as she grabbed my arm and pulled me to the floor. "We are about to see how much of a gangsta you are."

I was standing there as she started to circle around me doing one of these belly dances. I wasn't trippin' at all. In fact, she got me doing a little two step. I started feeling like I was back at home. We were having fun. It felt like we were at one of the slum clubs that we use to go to in high school.

The party was still crunk an hour later, but I was ready to go. I had seen everyone I wanted to see and had had way too many drinks up to this point. It was about two o'clock, and I was ready to hit the Spot. I was going to be looking for Amber, but I did want her to see me with Jody. She was sure to be at the Spot.

The name really wasn't the Spot. It was the Waffle House, but it was our spot. The Waffle House is where everybody went before going back to campus after a big party. There were a couple of them in town, but this one was the closest one to campus. There were sure to either be some fine females or a good fight at the Spot.

I pressed the issue of us leaving by closing out my tab. One last time around the hall and taking the traditional pictures and we were out the door. The let-out was almost impossible to leave. I had to go backwards out of the parking deck in order to dodge all the traffic.

"Where are we going now?

"To get something to eat. Why? You got somewhere else you have to be?" I said, breaking the tension that was growing in the air.

"Well there was this cute guy that I met . . . ."

"Ok, keep playing. See if I don't put you out right here."

"You going to put me out?" She said looking like I wouldn't do it.

"I would leave you right there on that curb. You could let that other guy pick you up." I gave her that look and placed my hand on her leg. "It's going to be ok," I finally said, giving her leg a massage as I watched her eyes start to close.

Everybody was calling as we pulled up at the Spot. A lot of people were already there so I told them to save two seats for Jody and me. I had my regular meal: pork chop and egg dinner. It was almost four o'clock, and I was getting sleepy. Amber never showed up, and I was not going to wait around any longer.

If I waited any longer, my boys would think that I was waiting on her. I would have to hear about that the rest of the night. Keith was there with his baby mama and Shawty had found some ugly-cute girl to go with. She was ugly but cute enough for him. We were talking about her in her face without her knowing all night. It was too funny.

It was getting late, so we left. This still did not solve my problem. The night was not over, and Plan A still had a chance. I tried not to think about it. The truth about the situation was that she was out with another man. I didn't know if they were drinking at the party or not.

Jody was getting in her freaky mode. We rode through downtown before heading back to campus. We had the top dropped and the skyline was beautiful. On our way back, Jody started to get loose in the car. She started to rub her hand around my thigh. I must have been dozing off because the car behind me started sounding their horn as the light turned green. Jody's hand went up my leg and then she grabbed my little man with both hands and started to stroke up and down.

At the next light, we put the top up and I pulled my pants down to my knees. I wanted her physically as I moved the seat back to a more comfortable position. This was tough. Amber had me messed up mentally, but this was feeling so good physically.

I was driving a Lexus around campus, not to mention a beautiful girl with her head in my lap. As we sat at another stop sign, I closed my eyes for a moment and tried to picture Amber and not Jody giving me head. What for? I didn't need Amber. Jody was fine and doing a lot more for me. I was trippin'.

Then my phone started to ring. I wasn't paying that phone any attention; it rang again and again. I reached over Jody and grabbed my phone from the middle console of the car. I was just going to turn the ringer off but I took a quick look at the name. It was Amber. I had to call back.

Jody rose her head up to ask me, "Who are you calling?"

"Making sure that Keith got back to his room safe because he had a little too much to drink," I told her. I was calling Amber back but the phone just keep ringing, and then the answering machine picked up.

"This is Amber, leave a message."

I was really fucked up now. I pulled into my reserved parking spot as we finally arrived back at the dorm. I didn't want to be on campus and run into Amber with Jody. I mentioned a hotel but Jody was already tired and didn't feel like going anywhere else.

I told her that I was going to get some candy from the vending machine. As I began to walk downstairs, Jody stopped me.

"Why don't you just go over there?" she said.

"Go where?" I replied acting like she was not talking to me.

"Just go see the girl. Don't play stupid . . . the one you were waiting on at the party, and at the Waffle House, and the girl that you love so much that you had to call her while I was trying to make you feel good."

"You knew?" I said looking for help.

"Yeah, but I love the fact that you are finally growing up. You are finally seeing that the world does not revolve around you. People have feelings too." She finished her statement by saying, "How long have ya'll been together?"

"Awhile, I guess." She knew I was being open with her because I would never tell the truth about another girl.

"Well if you are the same man that I use to be in love with, then I'm sure that she is still in love with you also. Just stop playing games and go and tell her how you feel." Jody stood there with a strong look on her face and meant every word.

So, I took one more look at Jody. "I'll be back," I said as I walked out the door leaving Jody by herself. Oh yeah, I took the Lexus, too. I was thinking of everything that I could say and things that I could do once I had arrived at her door. Should I get down on my knees, try to sing, or what? I was too much of a player for that, so I just went straight there with nothing but my pride to lose.

I'm here. Now what?

Who was this dude? Yeah I was looking in the window. I couldn't help myself. I had to know what I was getting myself into. I was jealous at this point and a little rage was building inside of me when I saw a male walking around her room. I had to knock on the door and tell Amber how I felt one last time. I just really wanted to know who this dude was.

Knock, knock.

"Hello," some guy said as he answered the door with a v-neck shirt on.

Without thinking I punched the guy in his face. Yeah, I snapped. I had to do something. I wasn't just about to stand around and allow someone to push up on my girl. I gave him a Menace to Society beat-down. Remember when Kane gave dude the beat-down outside Grandpas' house? It was like that. I was kicking him in the face and everything. He tried to get up, but I kept knocking him down.

"Get up!" I yelled over and over trying to get him to fight back.

Then I grabbed Amber like a G, and told her that I would never leave her side. This was one of my most poetic moments. I gazed into her eyes for a long period. I even heard music playing in the background. I bent her over backwards and gave her a kiss that made her forget that she was ever mad at me. It was almost like I was dreaming. I planned out what was going to happen, and I did it.

I was dreaming. I found myself back outside knocking on the door again, not giving the beat down to any buster or telling Amber how I really felt. Yeah, the thought sounded nice, didn't it? Well, this is reality. Things just don't happen like that. Everything is not always perfect. The good guy, or in my case me, does not always win, but he did answer the door when I knocked.

"Where's Amber?" I had to get firm with this guy because by the way dude looked, I didn't know if he wanted to buck or not. I had to let him know what time it was.

"What are you doing here?" she said as she approached the door. "You called me and then when you didn't answer. I decided to come by cause I didn't know what was going on."

"But it is four o'clock in the morning. Can't this wait until tomorrow?"

"Nawl, I got to get this off of my chest." Then there was a long pause as I gathered myself to tell her what I was thinking.

"We had something, I thought . . . but I messed that up. I know that," It was tough but I had to say it. "I felt something . . . more then I ever felt in my life, and it took me not having you in order for me to realize that I do want you. I mean, I need you. You are my other half."

"Can I say something?" Amber asked as I saw her getting emotional.

"Can I finish, please?" Then there was a brief pause. I had to bring out all the stops.

"For a week I have not been able to see you. For a week I have not been able to hold you. For a week out of my life I have not lived. I have missed a week out of my life because you were not with me, and I can't go through that week any more." I got that from an old song off the internet.

"Let me stop you," she said with a tear in her eye. "I'm not going to lie. I have been thinking about you, too."

"So, who is that man in there?" I had to clear up that issue quick.

"That is my cousin, and that is a she not a he."

I knew that it was something about that guy. I should have known that Amber would not have any interest in somebody like that. At first, I thought that he was a little funny, but now I can see clearly that no straight male would still rock a curl the way he did.

"I do love you, but I can't go through another week like you put me through. You didn't get all of the dirty looks that I got; the laughing behind my back; the finger pointing in the Café."

Amber then paused to gather her thoughts. "I can't even eat in peace anymore without someone asking if I'm all right. No. No, I am not all right. This hurts. I never felt the way you made me feel last week," she had to keep wiping her face as her voice began to get louder.

"You are the reason that I am not all right. You don't have everyone calling you stupid and telling you that you should have known. You don't care about me. You care about yourself."

The air became dull and uneasy as we both gathered our thoughts looking at each other, as if waiting to see who was going to say the next thing.

"You get all the praise for being a dog, and I get nothing but hurt," she continued. "I get looked down on for what you do to me. That's not love," she let me know.

"For some reason or another you chose to hurt me, and I can't be around someone that would hurt me." We stood there and looked at each other.

Amber was hurting inside, and I could feel it. She was really hurt. The pain of reality is the truth. She knew the truth now. The guy that she was putting her trust in was not respecting her moral values. She wanted to be loved, but by someone who she thought loved her just the same.

I had to think about everything that I had done. I was a bad boyfriend to have. Ok. Forget that. I was a bad boyfriend, period. Why was I even here? I was not ready for a relationship. She knew it, and knew what she was saying was true. I did not care about anybody and only thought of myself and my reputation.

I was looking for a token girl that would be under my arm when I wanted her to be. I wanted someone that was not in my face all the time, especially when it was something that I didn't want her to know about.

I must have got the wrong lesson in grade school about the birds and the bees. I mean, being around females is what I do. Why should I change how I act? People like me for me. I got cars, clothes, shoes, I'm handsome, and on top of all that, I got money. Who could ask for more?

"I'm leaving because I am wasting both of our time. I just wanted to say that I am sorry for everything that happened," I said as I walked off of the porch. I had come to realization that this wasn't going to work. I turned my back.

"Wait," I turned around and for a moment we glared into each other eyes.

"You going to church tomorrow?" she yelled out as I got to the street.

"Yeah," I really didn't know if I was, but I knew she was trying to find a way to make it work. The only thing that popped into her mind at the time was church.

"Yeah," she repeated, mocking me. "So, I'll see you there," she said as she stood there looking at me. She had a little smile on her face as if to say that everything was going to be ok. She closed the door behind her, leaving me in the street.

Amber was learning my ways and not allowing me to do the little things that I used to be able to get away with. She had become sensitive to the lack of respect that I was giving her. Not to say that she was becoming a player, but she was becoming a good coach. She was noticing change and adopting to the game.

She was learning as she lived. I was putting her in different situations. It was almost sad to say, but she was gaining an understanding of me. She even knew what I was probably going to do. I don't know if I was becoming too predictable. It was like she could see through me, but still love me for being me. This was one of the weirdest feelings that I ever had. A female that was learning and walking with me was becoming an eye opener.

Thank You

Amber and I started seeing each other again after that weekend of the Ball. It was good for a couple of days. Fall was settling a little early for us since we were a lot more north then normal. It wasn't snowing or anything like that. It was just a lot of rain and wet days.

I had gotten away from my pyramid and my ideology, to the point where stuff was all out of wack, I didn't care. Our time together allowed both of us to just be ourselves. We grew so close over the weekend that I even got a chance to smell her fart.

I had to straighten up in order to preserve my conjectures. I guess everything has to have a beginning and end. I was stretching myself too thin trying to keep up with all of these females. I couldn't keep this going too much longer.

I never thought in all of my life that my beautiful pyramid would begin to have missing blocks. Then I thought to myself. When things start to fall apart you are able to put them back in order the way you see fit. I started to change the game a little and added a key ingredient. It was called the "forget it" ingredient that must be taken in order to get back right. I took a night and called all of my chicks and told them I had a girlfriend. Some didn't care, and we were going to keep the party going. Others who thought they were next in line were disappointed and confused. Now the standards were set and the new line-up was posted.

The measure of a man is not if he makes mistakes, but if he learns from his mistakes in order to change. My pyramid, cell phone, haters, females, and friends all needed to be simplified. This was not a game anymore for me. My life was not a game. It was now reality. My life had become reality. A preacher once told me that *you don't appreciate life until you realize death is among you.* Well I felt like death came and went. This was my second chance at life. I had to ask myself, "what now?"

I thought about all my relationships and how they ended. Even though I said that I loved her, there were other things that I loved in my life such as football, my parents, and most of my friends.

What was I supposed to do about these people in my life? Was I going to put everything on the back burner just because I was in a true relationship with Amber? Even though Amber and I had been together a couple of months, college was a different world. This was just my first couple of weeks in college. Was I going to give up all four years of college for her? I had to think.

Later that night I called my Great Uncle Earl. He talked my ear off about how to handle females.

"See, a woman, a real woman wants a real man," my Uncle Earl told me. "No games. If you play with a real woman, she is going to become a player herself. Don't allow a real woman to even enter the game."

"Why Unk?"

"Have you ever heard the saying, when a good girl goes bad, aint no getting her back?" he said taking another puff from his cigar.

"Yeah."

"Well, it's true. Females are smarter than us. Don't teach them anything that you don't want them to know. That is game."

My uncle was old, but he still had game. I really never looked at it that way. There was so much I still had to learn, so we sat there on the phone for about an hour just talking about everything we could think of.

As soon as I got off the phone with Uncle Earl, the phone calls started. Every female in America was calling me. I didn't feel like I was cheating with the casual conversation. Well, they were not casual. Just a couple of innocent young females telling me about what they were going to do, and others talked about what they were going to be doing to me. Was this a form of cheating? Ya'll have to help me out. I am new to this.

I decided to come up with one of those Maslow's hierarchy of needs charts. I got rid of the safety, food, and shelter section. I grew up underprivileged so I knew how to make it through that part.

Self-awareness and belonging was at the bottom and loyalty and family was at the top. I tried the whole self-awareness thing that Maslow was talking about, and that didn't work. I had to adjust my life around something other than myself. That was not working because I was already putting everybody in front of Amber.

I couldn't see myself being one of those guys that as soon as they got in a relationship, start acting differently and stopped doing what they usually did. I was planning to have a healthy relationship, but the sleeping around part was my main problem. All of that was still a go in my eyes. How else was I suppose to find the right mate? I was taught to never go into a situation blind. If you don't check under the hood before you buy a car then you are going into the situation blind.

The weather had changed and so did the clothing. I could smell it in the air. Old meat, new meat, combined with lots of parties equals trouble. I figured that I had a couple of days in order to get straight before the weekend came. The majority of the crowd was going to be pulling in later in the week.

This week was going to be the biggest test of our relationship. I call the week after a couple gets back together *hell week*. Everything was going to be checked and rechecked to see if you changed. I hadn't called any of my other females over the weekend but was sure to run into all of them once I got out. I had to be strong.

There was one event that I forgot about that I knew was going to be trouble, the Phat Players Party. The Phat Players Party was heeled every homecoming and one of the most anticipated parties of the school year. It was the biggest party that lasted two days (Thursday and Friday). It would start Thursday night with a Step show and a party, breakfast, then a BBQ, a basketball game, and another big party downtown.

This was when everyone who was anyone comes back to campus for a weekend. No one was going to class because they just wanted to party. Plus, all of the females were in heat. I couldn't wait to see some of those female alumni come back. They always seem to liven up the party.

Wednesday was cool and peaceful until Casey tried calling my phone. She was calling back to back. After I didn't pick up, she tried calling from two other numbers. I turned the phone off and went straight to sleep. I forgot about waking up for the team meeting Thursday. I jumped out of my sleep at about 5:15 because I figured I was already late. I don't know why coach scheduled a six a.m. meeting. Coach said it was to see who was really dedicated, but I say he was just being a donkey.

I hadn't seen Bruce, but I knew he was somewhere around campus because all of his bags were in the room. I guess he went over to Jamie's room. I heard that he went and got a gun a couple of days ago. A teammate said that he'd been bragging.

It's simple. If someone gets a gun that means two things; either he is scared and was using it for protection, or he wanted to scare someone else. Well, guns never did scare me. I ain't never been no punk.

More importantly, I ain't stupid either so I had to watch my back. If you have ever been around a scary dude, you know that they react differently in certain situations. No man was around Bruce when he was growing up, so he always responded like a female. I wasn't even going to hurt the poor boy, but now he took it to a whole new level. I was not nervous about going to practice. I just had to know what I was getting myself into, kind of like hind sight being 20/20. I was using foresight.

I got over to the complex just in time for our team meeting. I was one of the last ones in the room so all eyes were on me. The coach gave me a look, and I took the nearest seat available. "Nice to have everybody here. The NCAA is having random drug testing this year. If I call your name, follow Tom down the hall and the others players will head to the weight room with Coach Speed." That was how coach started the meeting.

"Yeah right," Keith and I said looking at each other at the same time.

I was looking around not paying coach any attention. Bruce was sitting in the front row, sucking up like usual. He figured that if he acted like a ball player he would eventually become one.

Coach dismissed the meeting and neither me nor Keith's names were called to take that test. The weightlifting was quick and only took about thirty minutes to complete. Everyone was talking about going back to the dorm. I was going back to sleep. Practice wasn't until 2:45 pm and it wasn't even 7:30 am yet. I walked by the mail room once I left the complex to get my new schedule, like that mattered. I wasn't going to any class. Once I got back to the room I tried to go to sleep, but my phone kept ringing.

"Are you back?" "When are you coming to see me?" "What time are you getting up?" All these questions came from about sixteen different females during the course of my nap time. I should have just turned my phone off, but I also used it for my alarm clock.

I eventually got up and got something to eat before I headed back to the sports complex for practice. I really wasn't in the mood for practice, but I knew I had to or they were going to send me home. My phone started ringing. It was Shawty.

"You alive?"

"Yeah, but I ain't the one that ain't been in the room in two days."

"Man, I been caked up," he said quickly then jumped to his next statement. "Man, but seriously . . . I got a question to ask you." He sounded like it was going to be serious because his voice became real low.

"You know Leslie?" I didn't know why he wanted to know but this was my boy, so I couldn't lie. "Yeah, why what's up?"

"I might make her my girl."

"Cool, that's what's up." I was happy he found someone attractive that liked him.

"I need to know one thing," he continued to say.

"What's up?" What else did he need to know? "She told me that she knew you ... and I know that every girl you know ... well, you know."

I quickly responded, "Nawl, I ain't never touched her."

"Ok, I just had to make sure because you're my boy. I can live with anyone's leftovers but yours."

"What's wrong with my leftovers?" I said to shed some light on the situation.

"I don't live that porn star life. It's hard to convince a girl to calm down after you get a hold of her."

"You tripping. What's going on today?"

"Man, nothing. I'll be over there a little later on," he said with a little assurance that his girl was a lady.

"That's a B.E.T."

We talked the entire time it took me to get back to the football complex. I got dressed and was one of the first players on the field. My ankle was filling a little better, and I planned on having a good day of practice. I was moving around pretty good.

During practice Bruce and I didn't say a word to each other. We even went against each other in one-on-one drills and nothing was said. He caught one ball on me out of the five times that we went against each other. I wasn't really studying him, but I could tell he wanted to say something.

I knew he wanted to talk trash, but he knew better. Practicing football was like playing hockey to me. There was no telling when a fight would break out on the practice field. He held all his talking until we got back in the locker room. I was just sitting in my locker, and he walked by saying, "You know you can't check me," with a smile on his face. It was like the locker room was supposed to be his safe haven.

I let that one slide. I just sat there and tried my best to ignore him. Then Keith came from around the corner where Bruce's locker was.

"You know he is over there talking about you, right?" I thought Keith was just trying to start something but the look on his face let me know that he was dead serious.

This guy must not understand that I don't like him. Saying something like that was not making the situation better. Since he wanted a scene, I was going to give him what he wanted.

"You got something to say punk, say it to my face," I said as I was coming around the corner looking for trouble.

"You can't check me . . . all you do is hold."

"Shut up talking about football." I had to get to the point. "What is your problem?" I said loudly.

"You're my problem; you really think you got game? Females don't like you. They feel sorry for you. Please tell me that you were just joking about going to the league?" he was poppin' off now.

This buster really tried me, plus he decided to get up like he was a gangster. There were two things that I don't allow people to talk about, my parents and football. For Bruce to talk about my game was a slap in my face. I went right up to his face so that way he could hear what I had to say.

"Your dad should've pulled out and let you dry out on your mom's back. Don't come at me like that." There was a quick pause in my voice. "And that fake route that you think you caught . . . I quit on the play. Dummy," I wanted him to jump stupid.

"I wasn't looking stupid when I was getting with your girl Casey, now was I?" Why did he bring up the past?

I could have walked away, but that wasn't going to settle any-thing. I believe that fighting right away is the best way to resolve a problem. I swung and hit him again because apparently he wasn't getting the message that I was not afraid to fight.

Something was strange about the way he was acting, like he wanted me to hit him. He had a devious look in his eye. I didn't care. I was trying to kill this guy; all that mess he was talking and all the things he had done. He had tried me and I went off.

As everyone was holding me back, he went into his locker. Something told me not to turn my back but I did. Everyone was so busy trying to separate me that no one bothered to grab him so he had a clear shot to run at me.

I felt a sharp pain went down the middle of my back. The pain made my knees weak, and I fell into the players that were holding me back. I couldn't see for a moment. He didn't knock me out so the battle wasn't over. I was back up at him. I was messed up and couldn't see, but I was swinging. I didn't care who I was hitting. I turned around and saw him throw the object back into his locker through my blurry vision.

The fact that he didn't knock me out made me realize that he was not trying to kill me but wanted to fight. I squared up as if we were in the boxing ring. I could smell blood at this point.

"Come on. Come get some more." I couldn't see because my vi-sion was still a little blurry, but I was a fighter so he was going to have to kill me before I walked away from this fight.

"What is going on in here," Coach Tim said looking at both of us like we were fools.

"Nothing," I said with a mug on my face that let him know what was going on.

"Well since nothing is going on in here, then something is going to be going on outside . . . you two, get your things and meet me outside."

I took a step and felt faint. Blood started to run down between my eyes. My eyes closed. I couldn't feel my legs anymore. I had blacked out.

Final Thoughts: "If you knew the place you were going to die, would you be there? If you knew the moment you were going to die, would you allow it? My point is that no one knows, so make the best out of everything and respect life."

Chapter IX

WAKE UP

"Until you get up the nerve to ask the real question, you will never be blessed to know the real answer "

Why do you . . .

IT was 5:47 p.m. when my eyes opened again. I was in the hospital. I had 18 stitches in the back of my head. The walls looked cold, and there wasn't any carpet on the floor so I really wasn't even trying to move.

I wanted to leave, but I had to stay in the hospital until I finished my IV. I had lost a little too much blood too fast and had to be on one of those machines. Amber, Keith and Shawty were all there when I woke up. They hadn't noticed that I was awake so I just sat there and watched them as their eyes were glued to a new reality show that was on.

"I bet he wins," I said as my voice cracked like I hadn't had something to drink in five years. I was hungry and all I could think of was going to the Spot.

It wasn't any trouble getting up and leaving. Amber had my clothes in the same chair she was sitting in. She helped me put one piece on at a time. I was fine by now, but I still liked how she was putting on my clothes.

I was up and out of the hospital within thirty minutes. I never liked hospitals. It was called the practice of medicine for a reason. They are just practicing. I wasn't anyone's guinea pig.

Before we went to the Spot, I had to get something out of my locker. We drove back to campus from the hospital. My head was still hurting but my body was feeling good from all that medicine they gave me. We got to the sports complex, and I ran in to grab the things I left. There was no one inside. I stood in the middle of the locker room for about a minute and just looked down at the logo in the middle of the floor.

Then I went in front of my locker and looked at my picture of my family. I knew coach was about to send me home. I just wanted to play football. Football was really the only thing I had besides my family. I even thought about transferring back home to a state college. I didn't know what to do. All I knew was that this wasn't why I was here.

If I wanted to get pistol whipped and cursed out I could have stayed at home. I sat there for another minute and took about five deep breaths.

"Why?" I yelled out as I punched the locker.

It was seven o'clock, and everything was silent. I sat there for a moment. Someone had walked in. I could hear them walking around the back. I was about to leave so I walked around to let whoever know that I was ok.

I started yelling before I came around the corner. "They can't keep the kid down . . ." This guy had to be Lucifer himself.

It was just me and him. He turned around, and we stared at each other for a minute without words. Each of us were going over different situations in our head.

"What you doing here?" I didn't care at this point. It was just me and him.

"Look man, I just finished running so leave me alone," Bruce said.

"You want me to leave you alone? You must think this is a joke. Dude, I just got out the hospital and really don't care about if you want to be left alone," I said, my voice escalating.

"I'm not playing man, just leave."

"I ain't going nowhere. Who do you think you talking to? You had to wait until I turned around? What kind of female are you?" I was ready.

"What are you talking about? Don't nobody ever say anything to you . . . you are Mr. Perfect, the one that got all the girls, in all the papers and then for some reason thinks that you can treat people any way that you feel. Well forget you, all right?"

I just shook my head and looked at him.

"Do you hear yourself? You sound like a little female. What is this Mr. Perfect stuff? You can't be serious?" I wanted to know if he was really jealous of me: maybe not jealous but envious. For the first time, I could see the look on his face.

"You might just be the dumbest guy in the world. Look man, some of the things that you do you don't realize that you are getting me and a lot of other people in deep trouble," I said trying one more time to reason with him. "The incident with Amber and Casey, that could have been prevented if you weren't trying to show off. You made that way worse then it had to be."

"Nawl. What you mean is that you could still be with Casey if she didn't meet me," Bruce said, trying to boost himself up again.

"See, that's what I'm talking about," I stopped him right there. "You think that females rule the world. Everything that you do is about a female. There are a million females out there, and you try to impress each one. All you have to do is be yourself and forget these females," I said trying to talk some sense into the boy.

"You know what? You're wasting my time. If I told you how to get a chick, you would still have trouble. So forget it. Survive on your own," I was finished.

I started walking out the locker room. It was his life, and I left it as that. The floor had everyone's tape from practice still on it and I was looking down being cautious of where I was walking.

"Say something now . . . keep talking now . . . let's see how hard you are." I stood there with a tilt in my head because the gun was pressed against my temple. The barrel was warm as if it had been in his book bag all day. I wondered how much time I had before he pulled the trigger. Did I have time to move or maybe punch it out of his hand? Was it over and the only thing left to do is pray.

Then he lowered the gun quick and fell to his knees. My heart was racing as I leaned back on the door.

Bruce was on all fours crying at my feet. He was on the verge of murder and the thought of being a killer was eating him up inside.

I didn't know why, but I was thankful he didn't. He was in tears, and I didn't know what to say.

We sat there for another five minutes before anyone moved. I couldn't understand. Was this a calling for me or for him? Leaving the locker room, we looked each other in the eyes for the last time and went our separate ways.

I sat at the Spot quiet and didn't even bother to tell anyone what had happened. I guess they figured that I wasn't talking because of my head. That night as I lay in my bed, I thought about the last thing that he said. I never told him what he was doing. I would always blame him but he was just doing what he knew was right in his eyes. He had no idea what he was doing. I had to get out of here.

I'm going home. I grabbed a bag, threw some things in it, and head home for the weekend. I needed to get away, and there was no better place than home.

I reached the city about two in the morning, and I knew I wasn't about to walk in my mom's house that late because she slept with her pistol under her pillow. I wasn't trying to get shot. I called my God-brother Chancy.

Chancy was my God-brother and best friend. We grow up together and did everything as kids. When I went off to college, he stayed at home because he was a real street walker and never imagined following his dream. He never knew his father, but that never affected him. He always felt that he just had to grow up faster then everyone else. Whenever we would be off for the summer, Chancy would be the only one to get a real job. We played football on the same team all throughout middle school and high school. He kept me in line.

We always dreamed of playing Division 1 football at a big college together. I remembered how we mapped out what schools we were going to attend when we were in the 10th grade. Chancy just got caught up in some street mess that jeopardized his chance to get a big time scholarship. After that happened, he started getting to the money.

Getting to the money he was. I pulled up at his house, and it had to be at least thirty females over there with just him and about five or six of his closest homeboys. It was a big three bedroom/four bathroom house that sat on the hill. I loved being home. As soon as I walked in, Chancy gave me a big hug.

"Look who is here!" he said with a smile on his face that stretched from ear to ear. He was drunk and two females were holding him up as he was draped around their shoulders.

"Can you help me put some hair on my face?" he said to one of the two girls that were carrying him.

"Now how can I do that?" she replied.

"By letting me put my face between your legs." Everyone started laughing, and the girls were almost just as drunk as he was.

This was my dude. He never held back on telling a female what he wanted or how he wanted it.

"Mi casa, es su casa," he continued to say as they carried him away.

"What are you doing here?" my cousin Johnny said as he grabbed me from behind and tried to place me in a choke hold.

"You still weak and fat," I said as I got out of his grip without any effort.

"Only because I'm drunk. Ain't you supposed to be at school or something like that?" Johnny was just as drunk as Chancy, but he was so used to it that everyone thought that was how he really acted.

"Are you ever sober?" I replied staying away from the question he asked me.

"Sober? For what? You don't want to see me sober. I get angry when I'm sober. Let's have fun nephew," he said dragging me into the living room.

"I'm your cousin," I had to keep reminding him.

"I know who you are, Boi."

I started drinking and didn't stop until I found myself in the bathroom. I never should have taken that many shots of brown. The guest room had two girls sleeping in the bed, but that did not stop me from getting in with them. The room was right next to Chancy's master bedroom, and I could hear the walls shaking. He had about three girls in there with him so there was no telling what was going on.

One of the females seemed to be alive as I jumped in the bed. I didn't know them and they didn't know me, but all of that could be taken care of real quickly. I threw my arm across one of them and my leg across the other. Once they both started moving it was go time. I didn't even want to be in the middle because I wanted the two females to get to know each other a little better.

I don't know if they were drunk or not but as soon as they got together, they started kissing. I wasn't going to miss out on none of this.

I took one of the girl's underwear off and threw them across the room so she couldn't find them. After I realized they were down for a good time, I got loose.

"Wait. Lay this way," I turned one of the girls around so that the other girl had a chance to get pleasure from her. I was standing on the bed like King of the Mountain.

"This is how we do it in the South," I said proclaiming my crown. "Now represent where you from and don't disappoint anyone," I said falling down drunk with both of them landing on top of me.

"I'm from Houston," one of the girls said.

"Well howdy, cowgirl!"

"And I'm from the N.O.," the other said as she pulled back her hair and started giggling.

"Well, let's make it wobble wobble, shake it shake it, and round it up, cowgirl!" I was drunk but having the time of my life.

We went for about an hour or two with no limits. I eventually passed out after I got what I needed. It was great to be back at home. Chancy always knew how to show me a good time. I needed this. I slept like a baby.

I got up before everyone else. The two girls were in the corner of the room under a little sheet. It had to be about 7:45 am. I went downstairs to watch a little TV. Chancy must have heard me moving around and came down to see what was going on.

"You cook now?" he said as I was standing by the stove.

"I gotta survive," I said grabbing two beers out of the refrigerator and giving one to Chancy.

"There's nothing like a cold beer in the morning," Chancy said as he grabbed the remote control. "Ain't you supposed to be in school anyways?" he looked at me and said as if he was just realizing where he was.

"Man, I had to get away. They were trippin' so I had to come home before I kilt somebody."

"They getting you mad like that? I guess it's good I didn't go then. You know I don't play that." Chancy was real about being street. He didn't care about nothing when it came down to disrespect. The room got quiet, and we just sat there.

"Look man, I been getting into a little mess lately." Chancy started to say but then paused as if he didn't want to tell me.

"You straight?"

"You know I'm straight. I'm just telling you because you need to stay in school. It's getting crazy out here." He was serious, and I could tell that something had happened. I wasn't going to force him to tell me cause that's not a part of the Code. Only receive what is given. Never ask about the obvious.

"Stay in school, bro. I wish I'd had a chance to get away, for real."

"Don't start getting emotional on me," I said to brighten up the conversation.

"I thought you got someone pregnant."

"I did that, too." He let it slide out of his mouth like he already told me.

"You what? For real? Stop lying! By who?" I asked so many questions that I wasn't giving him a chance to answer the first one.

"Erica," he said as he took another swig of the beer.

"So, she finally got ya," I said, laughing at him because I distinctively remember him telling me, "I'll never get her pregnant."

"Do I need to cook?" some fine, tall, dark skin girl said as she came around the corner with no clothes on.

"Yes, baby. You know how I like my eggs, like you did last time."

"Ok," she responded, and walked in the kitchen to make him breakfast.

"Things will never change around here, huh?" he said as he looked at me and got up to go put on some clothes.

"Get dressed . . . we're going to the park."

The Park

The park was super thick. The park hadn't been like this in a minute. It was a nice day outside, and everyone was riding around in their old schools. I felt like I was at a car show. There were Cutlasses, a couple of Novas, a Malibu, and I think I saw an old school 66' Charger. Chancy was killing the game with his seven forty five BMW. It was burnt orange with the 24 inch matching shoes. He had new money.

We took a lap around the park before we parked on the curb right in the front. We sat in the car for a minute looking to see who everyone was. We never jumped out of the car fast. I reclined my seat and saw three females coming up on us.

"Is that Erica?" I asked Chancy.

"Who?" he said looking around real fast. He turned back around in his seat and slid down. "Act like you don't see her," he told me.

"Chancy," Erica started knocking on the window.

"You aint got no tint on your car. She can see you," I told Chancy. This guy was silly.

"I see you Chancy . . . why are you trying to play sleep?" Erica said as she came around the car, reached across me, and slapped him on his leg.

"What's up baby? I was just taking a little nap," Chancy said wiping his eyes like he just woke up.

"Get out the car, silly little boy, and give me a hug," Erica was fun to be around. She had a good spirit.

153

"Why are you home?" Erica asked me as she hit me in the chest. "You in trouble?"

"No. Why every time I come home I have to be in trouble? I responded to her question.

"Alright now, don't make me go tell Momma E." Ever since we were little she would always tell my mom what I was doing.

Erica was Chancy's girl for a while. They broke up like two months ago after being together almost four years. Everyone knew they were going to get back together because neither one of them went away to college. Plus, they had a baby on the way.

They were together almost our entire time in high school. They were the first real couple that went to take pictures together. They would come to school every other week passing out some pictures that they took. I have a shoe box full of their pictures. She was like my little sister because every time me and Chancy were together she was somewhere around.

Chancy and Erica were standing at the front of the car. She looked as if she was asking him a lot of questions. I knew what the conversation was about. They'd had the same conversation a million times. She probably wanted to know if he was talking to anyone else. Then follow it up with a lie about how much fun she has been having the past two months. They had broken up before and every time it was the same thing. Erica gave Chancy a hug, and he came and jumped back in the car.

"So when is the wedding?" I asked, being funny. I knew they were going to get back together.

"Nawl, I don't think that is going to happen." I could tell in his voice that he was serious about this.

"What? She cheated on you?" It had to be something serious because they had unconditional love. They had the kind of love that doesn't go away.

"You really want me to tell you what happened?" He sat up and got into his story telling mode. "I was lying there with her one night, and it felt like I was lying next to a stranger." He leaned back and took a deep breath thinking if what he said came out right.

Chancy looked at me and continued "I mean, I know you got females, but that one girl that you know you love . . ." he paused as he grabbed a medicine bottle out of his middle console. "I just couldn't feel the love anymore. It felt like I was just there, and she was there, but we weren't together," he finished as he reached in the glove compartment and grabbed a cigar.

"That's it?" I asked "So, you never caught her cheating or anything? You just couldn't feel the love anymore?" I was trying to find some reasoning behind this silly mentality.

"It sounded stupid to me at first, too. Now, I know what I did was the right thing," Chancy was quick with rolling and by his next sentence he was passing it to me.

"It got scary trying to sleep in the same bed with a person you didn't know anymore. We both know who we are now, and our goals in life are totally different." He looked me dead in the eye. "Look at me. I ain't going to no charity events and banquet where I have to dress up." He knew that Erica's folks had a little money and didn't want their daughter hanging around him. "I know you been at college letting them chicks sleep in your bed. You know you can't let no chick sleep in your bed." He was trying to flex on me because he knows I'm the one that told him to stop doing that a long time ago.

"What did she say out there?" I asked.

"Same ole' thing. Nothing. I don't think you realize, I was waking up five times a night just to make sure she wasn't doing something crazy."

There was this Junky that was trying to make some money dancing for the people on the street.

"Something like that," Chancy said making fun of the homeless man. "Let's ride," Chancy said as we pulled off headed downtown.

I spent the entire day with Chancy. We went to the mall, downtown, and then finished the afternoon off with three different girls over to the house. I didn't want to go back to school, but Chancy said that he was going to tell my grandma if I didn't.

I left Sunday night about six o'clock and got back in time to go by the Café and get something to eat. It was good that the Café stayed open 24 hours for the numerous scholars that burn the midnight oil. Everyone was walking out when I was walking in. Keith was among the crowd.

"You just got back?" Keith asked as we met in the door way.

"Yeah, you should have come. Chancy set it out back at the crib."

"So, what's up for tonight?" he asked as he looked at the group leaving. He had to be eyeing one of the girls.

"I don't know. First, I have to get something to eat. Then I'll just be in the room."

"Ok, I'll let you know if we do something." Keith wasn't really trying to do anything. He had his eyes set on what was about to happen. It was just the usual conversation that football players have with each other.

"Hey, Double Dog . . . thanks." Keith said before he turned the corner.

"For what?" I didn't know why he was saying thank you. I hadn't done anything.

"The talk we had really helped. Thanks."

"No problem." I guess he just wanted someone to listen. I was just there. It was nothing special. I just sat there and listened.

A couple of guys were still in the Café eating, but I still sat by myself. I called Chancy to tell him I made it back, but he didn't pick up. We had another real talk before we left that got me back up the road and back focused on what I needed to do. I finished eating my chicken sandwich and headed to the room.

The walk back to the room was peaceful and gave me time to talk to myself. There's nothing wrong with talking to yourself. If you can't talk to yourself, how will you ever know yourself?

I spent the next two days in the training room. I lifted weights in the morning with our strength coach and went to rehab during practice times. I even went to class, on time, Monday and Tuesday. I guess I just needed to go home for the weekend to get my mind right. I had to calm down and start living for myself just as everyone else seemed to do.

Those two days were peaceful and relaxing. I had dodged every conversation dealing with what happened last week and was trying to focus on getting back to being myself.

It was good to be back in my room and it was even better that Bruce wasn't around.

Then the phone rang. It was Shawty. "Hello."

"Get up and let's go. The AKA's are having a party, and we are going," Shawty said yelling into the phone.

"Man, I aint going anywhere tonight. I have a paper I have to finish."

"You didn't tell me you went to the crib, either. You know I woulda went."

"I needed to get away after everything that happened. I was about to go crazy," I said coming up with another reason for not going anywhere. I rolled over and looked at the clock. It was like almost twelve now.

"I know. I was there when you got out of the hospital, remember?" he was trying to be funny inferring that Bruce had put me out of commission for a minute. "Plus that happened two years ago. Let's get back to these females. Come on, get up," he said joking.

"You know I saw him in the locker room that night."

"Nooo," Shawty said coming through the phone.

"Ya'll got into it again?"

"Yeah, I'll have to tell you about it when I see ya," I said trying to get off the phone. He was already with a lot of people and talking loud.

"Let's get him. What are we waiting on? He's just trying you now." Shawty was ready for whatever at this point.

"He knows what time it is. I don't think he is going to be coming around me anymore . . . not after what happened in that locker room," I said to infer what I had to tell him later.

"Don't hold back on me like that, shawty. What you about to do?" He sounded like he was getting dressed and was on his way already, but I wasn't moving.

"So we aint going anywhere for real?" he said, trying to change my mind.

"Nawl, I'm just going to lay low and chill out tonight."

"Yeah whatever. Hit me up tomorrow."

"That is a b-e-t," I stated to end the meaningless conversation we were having.

There was something wrong with Shawty. I think I should have a talk with that kid about drugs. There is a time and place for everything, and he was using drugs, everywhere, all the time. He starting to get wild like me, and by him being a regular student they will put him out if he doesn't maintain a B average.

Then the phone rang again. It had to be Keith because he always calls after Shawty to tell me the exact same thing.

"I told Shawty that I am not going," I just blurted out as soon as I picked up the phone.

But it was not Keith. The phone was silent. I did not know who it was. They were calling from an Atlanta number, and I could barely hear what they were saying. I grabbed the remote and turned the TV down.

"Who is this?" I said strong trying to figure out who it was.

"Tina." I could hear a tear drop off of her cheek and automatically I knew that something was wrong.

"What's wrong?"

"Everyone is at the hospital," I could hear fear in her voice because she said it holding everything she had inside.

"In the hospital? For what?" I said getting mad at the fact that I was not there, and she was taking too long to tell me what was going on.

"Chancy has been shot."

The phone dropped out of my hand and fell in my lap. This wasn't happening.

"Who?" I said getting as I grabbed the phone. "What did you say?" I yelled.

"Chancy was shot," she said so softly that I could barely hear her. "We are at the hospital," she said instead of saying whatever she was trying to say.

"Tina, calm down. Who is in the hospital?"

"Chancy."

Tears of anger filled my eyes now, and I couldn't talk anymore. Tina was asking me questions like, "When can you leave?" but I couldn't speak. I could only listen. The only information that I was waiting on her to say was what hospital they were at. After I found that out, I hung up the phone by saying, "Don't let my brother die."

This was really eating me alive. I looked in the closet and grabbed my safe so I could pray as I rolled up. I never did unpack so I grabbed my keys and hit the road. Wait till I get there. I had to relieve some stress. Every time I exhaled, the gray mist that rose to my eyes had his face in it. I needed answers. This is my brother we were talking about.

Within ten minutes, I had jumped in the car and gotten about fifteen miles away from campus. I was on my way back home. I did not care about being tired or falling asleep on the road. I just wanted to be there for Chancy and everybody else. Why did I leave? He told me he needed help, and I left that man there with them lames.

I was not worried about spring practice, Bruce, or even Amber for that matter. I just needed to get home. I was focused on getting to the hospital and saving my brother's life. I just felt that if I was there, then none of this would have happened.

I was doing about 110 on the highway. I got there about three o'clock in the morning and went straight to the hospital. Tina, my mom, and all the members of Chancy's family were there as I entered the waiting room.

"Where is he?"

No one answered me; the room felt like death had come over everyone. I knew that Chancy was not dead. I asked again.

"Tell me. Where is he?" I looked around but got no response. "Can someone please . . . please tell me where he is?" I said raising my voice in anger then realizing that no one was answering me for a reason.

Tears began to come down my face as I headed towards the double doors to find my brother. My mom, who was seated the closest to the door, caught me.

He was gone. The air pressure in the room got so heavy that we both fell to our knees. There was nothing that I could do.

Everything that mattered in my life was gone. I was fooling myself thinking that things were going to change. Nothing was going right. I felt like killing someone. I only wanted to know who did the shooting. "Who did this?" my faced was tight as I held everything inside.

"Why ma, why, why my brother . . . ?"

"I don't know son, I don't know."

God help me. Who did this? Father tell me. This wasn't making any sense to me. Who was with him? Where were they at? How come one of them didn't get hit? "AAAAAAhhhhhhh." I yelled as loudly as possible. This was my brother. Who was I going to talk to? Who was I going to tell my problems and talk about females with?

Thoughts of revenge filled my head. I already had a couple of groups in mind. I knew where to go to get what I needed to correct the situation.

There was this one time, this summer when we got into a shoot out with some dudes on the East Side. I think I remember seeing them at the park. I didn't care who it was. They better not let me find him.

Tears were streaming down my face, and everyone was filled with pain and anger that was too deep to experience through words. I kept asking "Why?" but each time the response expressed was, "It was just his time to go."

"Stop saying that. We talkin' about my brother here. It was not his time, and I know that for a fact." I hated to talk like that in front of my people, but I couldn't hold this in.

"It isn't his time to go," I yelled as I broke free from my mom. "No one can tell me that it is his time to go. It was not his time, not like this, and not right now."

Just Talking

I found myself sitting in my car with my pistol on my lap. This was killing me now. My grief turned my tears into blood which gravity pulled away from the terror in my eye. My bloodshed eyes closed as I went into a sudden silence. My soul escaped my body and went to a place of tranquility. The blood still pours as if I had thousands of puncture wounds on my face. I thought that the pain would come out as I sat outside and talked with my God. I confessed my deepest secrets in exchange for a response, but there wasn't one. I was alone.

I went all the way back and talked about the things we did when we were young. I was trying every option. I found myself in my car without any tears left. The sun was coming up, and everybody was starting to head home from the hospital. I saw the faces of everyone that were leaving, but they didn't see me. I reclined my seat back and I decided to take a nap right there in my car. I thought about how I'd rather it had been me to die in that locker room than have to see my best friend like that.

The clouds were moving at the same pace of the world. I wasn't thinking about anything: Phat Weekend, Homecoming, the season, or anything that had to do with that University. I wanted to get far away from that place. Nothing good was coming out of my college experience. People were being hurt, football wasn't working, and I felt like I needed to be home with my family.

I knew he had got shot so I started thinking about images of him sitting at the house and a car driving by. At first slow, and then I could feel how they began to roll down the windows. The shots pierced holes in his skin as he tried to escape the bullets coming at him. I could feel myself there helpless and unable to help anyone. I started to feel guilty about not being there. BANG, BANG, BANG. I thought that I was dead. Tina was knocking on the window.

"Can you take me home? I rode over with Kia, but she is tired and is about to go home. I'm not ready yet."

"Yeah, just let me know when you're ready."

"Ok," she stated as she went back inside.

It was only about twenty minutes before she was walking back out. My chair was reclined just enough so I could see Tina coming. "You ready?" she said as she came across the street. The sun was trying to peak through the clouds but they were much too thick for that. It was a still morning that had the presence of death. The wind wasn't even blowing.

I leaned my chair up and then reached across to open the passenger door. "Yeah . . . you hungry?" I hadn't eaten since yesterday, and my stomach was letting me know.

"I know you can eat, fat boy. You gettin' big. What are they doing to you up there?"

"You know, the same ole' thing. Working out, sleeping, having relations: the basic food groups."

There was no one at the Spot when we got there. We had to get some breakfast before we went to her house. I was hungry and felt like talking to someone that knew what was going on. We sat for a minute quiet before she started to tell me about what happened.

"He was just sitting there on the phone," she started. I couldn't cry anymore. I just wanted answers.

He was sitting at the red light and a car pulled up beside him and tried to rob him. Everyone was saying, that Chancy wasn't going. He started bustin' at them, and they shot out the back window and hit him in the back of his neck as he got down the street. Tina said that he hit one of them. No one knew where they'd taken him.

"The messed up part is that Erica was on the phone with him and heard everything. I can't imagine having to hear that." Tina then told me that Erica was going to have a girl now and was three months along. I was going to have to be there for the child now. I was going to be there for them as if they were my own.

"Where was she?" I asked.

"Getting her nails done. You know how she gets when she can't deal with a situation."

It's nice talking to Tina. She'd always had good conversation. She was silly like me and could find a little life in everything. Then Tina's phone rang.

"Hello. They do? Ok," I could tell it was about the shooting the way she was looking at me.

"They have someone," she said as she hung up the phone.

The police already had a suspect in custody, which was good they did because I was going looking for answers in the morning if they hadn't found anyone by the time I got up. My uncle works for the Police Department so I knew that they were going to beat him when they got him behind those jail bars.

Then our conversation moved from sad to pleasant. We started talking about how each of us were doing and what we had done. Tina had graduated with me but decided not to go to college. Instead, she saved all her money and had opened her own clothing line during the summer. She told me about everywhere she had been the past couple of months: Paris, London, and Milan. I was proud of her.

I forgot to tell ya'll, me and Tina had a past relationship if you hadn't figured that out yet. We went together in the tenth grade, and she cheated on me with the new guy. Yeah, it was one of those things. She actually fell for the new guy. When that didn't work-out, I was in another relationship. So she's been around, and I still have feelings for her. You could say that she made me the man that I am today.

I had to call my mom even though I'm grown because it was the right thing to do. I also called my coach and told him about what had happened. I wasn't going to be back for the rest of the week, and I thought he should know. It was about seven o'clock now, and I was almost sleeping at the table.

After breakfast we went back to her house, and I fell asleep on the sofa watching TV. I did not want to go home because I knew that everyone would be over there. I needed to get away from everyone for a while.

I kept tossing, turning, and talking in my sleep. Tina came into the living room and woke me up a couple of times. She said I was starting to scare her.

"Go get in the bed." She was up so I took the bed to get a couple of good hours of sleep in.

It had to be five in the evening before I was awakened by the smell of pork chops and greens. Tina had cooked dinner, but the bed was so comfortable it was hard to get up.

"You eating?" she said as she came into the room to wake me up.

"Yeah. What did you cook?"

"Pork chops, greens, and macaroni and cheese. I learned how to cook when I was in Italy."

"They don't cook greens and fried pork chops in Italy," I told her, speaking in an Italian accent and joking.

"It's nice to see that you still have your sense of humor." She put my plate down as I sat up in the bed. She turned on the TV and got in the bed with me as we sat there and ate.

Dinner was good. Since it was just the two of us, I had seconds. After eating dinner, we made our rounds. We went by Chauncey's mother's house and stayed for a couple of hours. We went by my house and then to a couple of friends' before getting tired of hearing everyone cry. Eventually we got back to Tina's house around twelve o'clock.

Final Thoughts: "I use to look my haters in their eyes to let them know I see them. I don't look anymore . . . . I know they are watching me . . . . Now I keep my hand on my heat to make sure they know I'm waiting."

Chapter X

BREAKIN OLD HABITS

"Destiny is revealed to each individual as they reach that given moment in time. Comprehending related historical events should aide in building your future. Stop allowing history to repeat itself. We are killing ourselves"

Say NO

"I'M tired. I'm about to get in the shower and go to bed," I told Tina as we walked in the door.

"The towels are in the closet and don't use up all of the hot water," she responded as she went in the kitchen to get something to drink.

The water felt good, and she had a shower radio so you know I was in the shower jamming to myself. I didn't want to get out. It was just more relaxing letting the water hit my back; not wanting to face the world again. Then the curtain flew back, and Tina jumped in.

"You scared?" Tina said as she got in the shower with me.

"You almost got punched. I didn't know what was going on. You could have been a robber." She did scare me, but I wasn't about to tell her.

"You were taking too long, and there wasn't going to be any hot water left. Move over and pass the soap."

I had taken a shower with her before but that time the lights were off. I was trying not to touch her but that was virtually impossible. Her backside was sliding against me and her caramel skin had a Krispy Kreme glaze from the steam. The way the water rolled down her skin made me want to taste her. I leaned closer as she had her back to me.

"I got soap in my eye," I said in a panic.

"I can't see." Tina had slung her freshly soaped hair in my face. Tina had to grab me before I knocked both of us out of the shower. She took control and grabbed me by the waist and pulled me under the water with her.

"Hold your head under the water," she commanded.

"Ok, but you are trying to drown me," I said. It felt like I was under a fire hose.

Afterwards, she handed me a rag to wipe my face. I could see how the water was gently ascending down her face. We stood in the shower face to face. Her eyes were beautiful. I began to rise as her thighs made a crease with femininity liquefied flowing for my appetite. So I placed myself between her legs. As she walked forward I took a step also. Then she took a step forward, and I slipped out. She grabbed the soap and took a step backwards as I didn't move. She arched her back as I slid back in.

Two long strokes later, I pulled out. I thought about what was about to happen as I somehow seemed to keep playing around and getting a couple of strokes in as we kept moving around the shower taking each of our souls through the mouth.

I had to get out. I didn't have any protection, and I knew it was about to go down. I grabbed the towel and started drying off, when the force of a wet body threw me on the bed.

I didn't want to have a setback. I was doing good with Amber. Forget it. I'm hurting and this is the only way I know how to fill this empty space in my life. If she is down, then I am, too.

This was something that I could not say no to and sure wasn't going to either. There wasn't anything that would make me stop this time. It started first with a little kissing, soft and passionate.

Then we somehow found ourselves bodies flipped opposite on the futon couch in the living room. We were making our way around the house.

I knew she was wild as I threw her against the bathroom door. She continued to take everything I was giving her. Her legs were long and were wrapped around me as I sumo-walked from room to room, throwing her up each time to keep the beat going.

The warmth of her body was what I needed. I needed her right now. We ended up back in the bedroom. She turned around and put her knees on the bed and looked over her shoulder. She wanted me just as bad as I lusted for her. Our bodies met in rhythm.

We moved slow at first, and then picking up the beat as if we were playing the drums. She was feeling on me as well as herself. We were making every second feel like a minute and every minute feel like forever.

"Be gentle," she said softly.

I turned her over and placed her on her back. The passion became more intense as the strokes became longer and slower. She began to rub on my back as I held her by the back of her neck making sure that she felt every motion.

Our obsession with one another grew as we started to move and break objects that were in the room making the climax that much better. Our two bodies felt every inch from head to toe; kissing, licking and caressing every part to make the entire body feels relaxed and comfortable.

We fell asleep in each others arms and forgot about everything that was happening. All of the pain that once was the center of attention was placed on the back burners for this moment in time. Lying in the bed, I began to realize that life is what you make of it. It is too short. Many people don't realize how short life is until they are confronted by death, the taker of life.

I was only nineteen and didn't know anything about death or what it held. I was living for the moment and was concentrating on survival. I just wanted to live.

"Ring."

Homecoming

"Hello," I said without looking at the phone before I answered.

"So you just don't call anyone anymore?" it was Amber

"I had to," I said, still asleep.

"You had to? What kind of answer is, that?" "You don't call or anything in two days . . . what is that about," she continued thinking I was still on campus.

"Calm down." I sat up on the edge of the bed. "Chancy got shot, and I had to come home," I said trying not to wake Tina.

"You can't call and tell me something like that? You just left me here." There was a long pause as she gave me time to think about what she had just said.

"Even though I only met Chancy once, I . . . I still want to be there." I had hurt her, again. She was right. I did just leave.

"Are you ok?" Amber asked. I hadn't said anything for a minute. I was just allowing her to talk.

"Yeah I'm straight. The funeral is tomorrow and then I guess I'll be back at school."

"What do you mean you guess?" Amber asked, as I sounded not too confident about what I was saying.

"Well, I wish you had told me. I would have been there with you," she said sounding concerned.

"I didn't know until I got to the hospital. He was gone when I got there." Once again there was a long dark pause in which neither one of us said anything.

"Well, call me in the morning. I was just worried . . . Why?" Amber was stern. "Talk to me. You can tell me things. Stop leaving me in the cold all the time." She wanted to be a part of what was going on in my life, but I had to deal with this one on my own.

"Ok."

"I'm serious. Don't play with me. You better call." Amber was concerned, and I could hear it in her voice.

"All right," I replied as I hung up the phone and went back to sleep.

Life was confusing, and I was just playing it out. I realized that I had no clue about what I wanted to do in life with females or anything else.

What am I really going to do with myself? My lies were easy to tell but just becoming meaningless to keep up with. I was getting a headache. Forget everything and everyone. Forget my theories and rules. There was only one rule that mattered at this time: by any means necessary.

The day of the funeral was misty. It was slightly overcast and the older women had on their furs around their neck. The day had a cold wind but not cold enough to stop anyone from coming. It had to be at least a couple hundred people inside the sanctuary and another couple of hundred that couldn't get in. I got a chance to see a lot of people that I had not seen in a while. The whole hood was there and bro had the females so you know most of them showed up. All of our old coaches, teachers, and principal were there. Since we had only been out of school for a semester, most of the community was there because everyone knew who Chancy was.

He had an open casket because he was shot in his chest and stomach. I thought it was going to be hard seeing his body. As I got closer to Chancy, I saw that he had on his high school letterman coat. I smiled. Tears were coming out but they were joyful, and I knew he was in a better place.

I don't know who let Uncle Roy do the prayer. He kept forgetting what he was saying and had to repeat himself over and over.

It's funny that people grow closer when someone leaves them. I guess it is one of those things where people don't know what they have until they don't have it any more. There were a lot of people at the funeral that were pregnant, too. The birth of life and the birth of death all in the same place. I guess that everything has a beginning and an end.

The funeral came and went. Just like life, it comes and it goes. It was painful as hell to sit there and see my boi in that casket like that. It was even more painful to see all the fake people inside the church crying like they were really hurting. The Repast after the funeral, turned into a little reunion for me and a Homecoming for Chancy. It was nice, though. He would have liked how he went out. All the big homies were blazing at the grave, and we stayed out there for hours after everyone else left. Everyone was headed to Chancy's mother house before we would hang out down the street at the park.

"So when are you going back?" Tina asked as we walked to the car. "I don't know." I was at a loss for words. It had gotten late, but there was enough light once we got to the park to continue until about eleven o'clock. Tina and I were posted by her car while everyone else was in little groups of about five drinking and talking amongst each other.

"Are you going to be ok?" Tina said as she grabbed my hand and squeezed it to let me know that she was going to be there for me. "I don't think so," I said looking up at the stars with my mouth wide open.

"You're not going to do anything stupid are you?" She wanted me to tell her my plans but I really didn't have any idea about what I was going to do. "I really don't know. I know I need to go back to school. I know I need to get focused on football. But . . . ," I had paused due to the fact that I didn't know where to go from there. "I just don't know," I finished saying as I got up and started skipping rocks off the top of the lake.

"You don't know what?" Tina said. She continued, "I don't know why you do this to yourself. You know what you have to do . . . you just don't know why." She looked at me. "For yourself, do it for yourself. You know that everyone looks up to you. Everyone, everyone except you."

I had nothing to say. He words were true, and she continued to speak them, "You have everyone supporting you, but you are not supporting yourself." She stood there next to me. "Just keep living," she said as we started walking along the edge of the lake. The lake at the park was peaceful and still.

"Being ignorant is not hard. I don't know why you try so hard to blend in when you were born to stand out." She was digging in deep now. I had to respond, "I tried to just live. I have tried to enjoy life . . . but how can I, when I don't even know why I'm here. We are not here to enjoy life. If that was so, then why can't I live how I want to?"

"You can. Listen, I don't want to argue with you. I love you. I just know you can achieve so much if you just stop playing so many games." Tina was right but I couldn't tell her that. We had made a complete lap around the lake and headed back up to the house where everyone was at.

We both sat there and ate the rest of the chicken wings. We started a different conversation, but the fact still remained the same. I had to stop playing this game.

I had to get back to school and also tell Amber what was going on with me. I was not ready for a serious relationship, and I knew it. I still had two hundred females' numbers in my phone. What kind of boyfriend was that? I was not going to tell her about me and Tina. That would only make the situation worse. I just decided to tell her that I was not ready for a serious relationship.

In order to rebuild, complete destruction had to take place. I was changing the game alright. In order to grow, I had to understand that I was now in a different situation. I had to reorganize.

I just wanted my life back. I had to tell myself I could handle this: refocusing my attention on myself and gain control over this situation. Come on, I was the man. I couldn't let this get to me. I slept at Tina's house once everyone left. I slept in her bed, with her, again. I woke up in the middle of the night and headed back to school.

It wasn't easy once I got back to school. Everyone was asking me about what happened, but I really didn't want to talk. I hid out in Amber's room for about a week. She was making me dinner every night to make sure that I wasn't out drinking.

I had to wait until the right moment to tell Amber that I needed some time to be alone. I finished lifting weights and went over to her dorm room. My phone began to ring. It was Tina, but I didn't have time to talk to her.

"Hey, I'm going to call you right back," I said rushing Tina off the phone.

"Make sure that you call me back because I have to tell you something important." She didn't sound upset. I had something else to do.

"Ok-key-do-key, will do." What did she need? Tina only called me when something was important.

I had to get this off of my chest. I was not going to turn back or forget what I was going over to her room to do. She did not need me in her life. It was time for me to stop being selfish and let her go.

Knock, knock.

"What's up? I was just about to call you." She came to the door wearing those college shorts with the school logo on the back.

"Amber we need to talk," I said as I grabbed her hand before she could walk into the back room.

I chose to talk at her house because I was going to be the one that left after it was over. What would I look like calling her over to my room and then making her walk back? I did have a heart. "What's up?"

"I want you to realize why I am telling you this first. My life is not together. I really need to get myself together," Then I just stood there for a minute.

"What are you trying to say?" she said trying to look me in my eyes.

Words were built up inside of me and came out all at once. "Look at me. This is not how I want to live. This is not me. This is not who I really am. I don't know who I am."

"So, is it over or what?" she said with a firm tone in her voice.

My thoughts were racing because I wanted to tell her I was just playing around and continue with my confusion, "I just need some time by myself," I said rubbing my head.

She had a puzzled look on her face, "Is this because of Chancy's death, because after a . . ."

"No, no, no," I had to interrupt. "Well yes and no. I mean I am nineteen, and I don't even know who I am. My whole life has been defined by how I looked, played football, and who I was with. I have let everyone define me in my past. I need to define myself. I just don't feel like hurting you while I find myself. I do love you. I love you enough not to want to hurt you, and the only way I can see that happening is . . . . ." I couldn't finish for some reason.

"Is it someone else again?" Amber was just asking questions now. She wanted to know the basic answers: with who, where, and why.

"No, and don't start that. Please don't start that."

"Then why are we really having this conversation. Tell me the truth?" she wanted answers, but I had said them all.

"I will be there for you, and I am going to need you to still be there for me. I just don't think that we need a title," I said while I was getting up and approaching the door.

"Tre," I stopped as I reached the door.

"I don't think I can do this anymore," she said. I didn't turn away. I looked at the door knob and took a deep breath. "I'm not going to let you keep taking me up and down," she sat down on the couch as her eyes glazed over.

"Please don't come back. It's becoming too painful." Amber was through with me. I could hear it in her voice as she got back up and went to the back room, leaving me standing there.

"I still love you," I said under my breath as I turned the knob and walked out of the door.

Walking back to my room, I never turned back to see if she was watching or following. I knew I had to move forward. Amber had learned the game. She was serious and expected me to take our relationship as just that, a serious one.

Amber was still a part of my life, but she did not have the label of my girlfriend anymore. All that I just went through would drive a normal guy insane. I wouldn't have changed a thing that happened. It taught me a lot about life that I did not realize. Many of my decisions I have to admit were selfish. If I didn't look out for myself, then who was I suppose to blame?

Finally. It's Over.

So I found myself lying on my bed at 3:54 a.m., thinking about this crazy mess I had gotten myself into. I was still in my first year of college, and it was hell. Just as I had an introduction, I had a conclusion, and just as I had a plan, I had obstacles.

I needed to do a lot to get back right, but first I needed to start over. I took a thirty minute shower and cut all of my hair off. My dreads were touching my shoulders and felt like they were holding everything that I had gone through. A fresh look is always a good start. Looking in the mirror, I could see that everything was going to turn for the best.

I had become wiser and did not even realize it. I started with a pyramid that eroded and weathered leaving a sand dune. The foundation was still firmly grounded but the visual aspect had faded just like my new hair cut. Humility came upon me as I stared at my new beginning and looked down at the years of worry that once set upon my shoulders.

I had to reevaluate my ideas and theories; my teaching, leadership, company, and my practices. I was at a changing point in my life. Amber had brought me to a stage in which the definition of love was misinterpreted. Words are complicated and have many different meanings. Love, for example, is based on attraction and seduction if used properly. Out of context many use the word love to express a lasting feeling that precedes an act. Without relations, love is just merely lust, an infatuation stage in a relationship.

Something was bringing about negative energy. I was busy trying to find a mate for myself when I should have been building a temple for my future. I was no longer thinking about my brothers and sisters but focused on selfish attributes. I was not living to my potential and becoming ignorant in the manner in which I illustrated my knowledge. I had to get back to being me. Living my dream and not placing myself in a position in which I was dependant on a female. I didn't need a soul mate. I needed to find my soul. Without a soul, I was merely searching for another body.

The game had not changed. I was just moving on to a more advanced stage. My audience had gotten bigger, and I had to pay more attention to the little things I was doing. Everything I'd learned had helped me up to this point, but now other rules and theories had to take place in order to help me advance even more. If I didn't learn, then I hadn't grown.

Plus, there was no telling how long I was going to be attractive. Ok, now I am just talking crazy. I will always be attractive. For real, things change which people have to realize. People's emotions and passions for certain things fade along with many other things in life that may mean something one day and nothing the next.

The game was the same. The game will never change from how I see it. Everyday that you decide to get up out of the bed you are involved in the game. The game of Life. Neither I, nor you, nor anyone for that matter, can change the course of life. No one can change the game. If people would just let things in life happen, then they would be more open to change when things don't go their way.

Ring.

It was Tina again. I forgot to call her back. It must have been important because it was 3:56 now.

"What's wrong?" I said instead of hello because I knew that something was wrong.

"I'm pregnant."

I GUESS THE GAME HAS CHANGED NOW, huh.

Final Thoughts: "Just say thank you. Wake up everyday and say thank you. You only have one life to live, whether you are in college, out of college, single, or married. It doesn't matter. You only get one shot at life. If you don't get anything else from reading this, understand that people are going to hate, so be yourself and do what you have to do in order to survive. Time is consistent and will tell your story. Hardship shows in your face and anger comes out when you speak. Change your mentality in order to change your LIFE."

Chai'

MEET THE STORYTELLER
Chai

Long before Man could stand upright and technology was introduced. People communicated nonverbally. Hands were like lips and to touch a woman was sinful. Every girl from the age of twelve was wrapped in preparation of becoming a wife. My God had promised the men of my kingdom that if we lived by his law, all our wives would be beautiful beyond all exceptions on the night of the wedding. So, my life is full of stories and one that is quite funny is the one about my wedding day.

I was young, rich, and famous to all the Neanderthals and decided to get married. I asked My God to send me a woman worthy of my kingdom. In walks a man with his daughter and speaks on her behalf. "My daughter is very beautiful and will fulfill every need as your wife." The man says to me.

So I'm going along with the whole notion that I'm about to marry this fine girl. On the day of the wedding I lifted up the vail, to present my wife to everyone. Everyone fell out laughing. She was so ugly. People were throwing stones and everything else they could find in the cave temple. That's where "getting stoned on your wedding day" came from.

After that, we got back to the cave, and I had to find a way to get rid of this ugly wife that God lied about. I thought I would out-smart God. I made her write on the walls in lamb blood that if she was ever viewed by another man I could leave her and marry again. She said "cool".

That evening I had all the Nomads come over. They were on their way up north and had to travel right by the cave on their way out the city. I told them I had some live entertainment for them. As they waited outside, I ran in and hid behind the rock. Soon as I got a spark of fire from the stick, I ran around screaming at the top of my lungs. FIRE. FIRE. My wife ran out the cave and all the Nomads saw my wife unwrapped. As the laughter came, so did the rain.

The Nomads left and ran into the woods leaving my wife in the rain, naked. I stood there calling for her to come in out of the rain but she remained until the last drop was out the sky. "Are you happy now?" she said as she entered the cage.

"NOT AT ALL" I said. She was beautiful. The rain had washed all the ugly away and standing in front of me was the most beautiful creature I had ever seen.

"I must leave you now, for I have broken the covenant of your house," she said wrapping herself.

"You ain't going nowhere. You think I'ma let you walk out of here. You can leave all that wrap off, my wife." I tried but nothing worked. She was exiled.

My God punished me for not believing in him. That's why all men now view every woman by face in search of the perfect wife. Until man realizes that beauty is from within, he will divorce every wife that he marries. Now, at first, I was mad he made me the example for generations but now it kind of cool. Take my mistakes and learn from them. It doesn't make sense for everyone to make the same mistake. Come up with new ways of being wrong, but that was in my younger days.

New ideas and new thoughts are what keep us moving forward and achieving great accomplishments. In looking at ourselves, the greater being comes from the temple that everyone has inside them, believing in the unbelievable. As a person becomes more in touch with themselves and gains an understanding of their purpose, they become three-dimensional. The unknown, or should I say to reveal the truth, is what keeps people from exploring and discovering the truth behind reality.

The reality is that this is Earth, the place between Heaven and Hell. We are living every day with demons and angels that influence our decisions. Most people would call it their "conscience." Forces and energy are what causes reactions and instincts, which allows a person to survive or die.

Knowledge is a very powerful word that is often overlooked by society. Insight comes from knowledge. Knowledge of the past and seeing a situation arise before others aides a person in all situations. In this, remember that the control over some persons mind is way more powerful than controlling that person's pocket. When you control a persons mind, their pocket no longer becomes a factor in what that person is capable of doing. I wipe my butt with my money. It's useless.

For clarity, vision is 93% sight, and the other 7% has to deal with comprehension of the situation. Many people can see but don't know what they are looking at. We as people have to move past merely describing and start illustrating.

Most people are considered smart by standardized test that are designed past upon a person's comprehension of society. The problem is that for a child, society changes every state, city, town, hood, and street. Most inner city children learn different tactics for survival in relationship to the suburban life style. The perception of society is different, but the tests are the same. Does that make sense?

I once asked a man to choose between money and power. The man then replied "Money." When asked "why" he repled, "Because money gets people power." Then I thought about it and decided that was the stupidest thing I have ever heard in my life.

My logic behind a person that would think like that is basic. If they use money as their primary goal to obtain other things that will make them happy, they will be sick all their days. Money comes and goes. You should build your life around something stable such as moral values. In looking at the other side, if a person with power took control over a situation and gained financial resources, then that person will continue to grow along with his power and money.

My life is not complete, and I will never know the true meaning of why I'm on Earth until my final moments. In the meantime, I am in a consistant pursuit to find the truth not happiness. My research is a collection of experiences and stories told to me. My logic of life can only come from my experiences and should be looked at as just that, my interpretation of my experience. In this, history must repeat itself and reveal the truth. As it is unfolded to me, I am gaining a greater understanding for life.

Life and time only have one course and that is to move forward. Why waste time when it will run out? I have a lot of stories to tell you so listen out. Most of my life, I've been sitting back listening and now I'm speaking out. Write more to understand comprehension skills. What I'm saying is let's figure out what's wrong and get it corrected. Too much time is spent talking about what's wrong. We know what's wrong. We the people are the problem, the solution, the question and the answer all in one. Don't be afraid to follow the Golden Brick Road. Welcome to God's City.

MEET THE WRITER
C. L. Thompson

I F I were to make a movie about my life until this point, I would entitle it "Watching the Grass Grow". This was my mentality towards life. I had lost all fight. I had started to watch the grass grow along with letting my life disappearing. My stride for becoming great was locked behind cell walls. I looked in the mirror one morning and my face was full of hair. This became my reminder of time. Physically I was able to withstand great pressures when psychologically not being able to caprice with humility.

I graduated from Frederick Douglass High School in Atlanta, Georgia (2G1), and went on to Vanderbilt University in Nashville, Tennessee. My time in school was well spent, and I made great strides at becoming a well rounded individual. The dream of going to the NFL clouded my potential of being a talented scholar.

So yes, I'm from the west side of Atlanta, Mosley Park to be exact. Yes, I was present during the era in which many American idols were raised. Understand that – "Ones true identity is no more than a characters if found away from home. There should be no conflict if the truth is told". If conflict arises then there is a liar present. The one who has to proclaim himself king can never see himself as a servant's son. Kings are crowned by the elders not proclaimed by the youth. You can't defeat me, so don't buck back.

The purpose in which this book was written was for me to overcome my personal battle with literacy. Unknown to many, I had been struggling with my reading for many years. Now, I have taken my personal time to understand literature. The origin of words, sentence structure, and verb agreement were all areas that I needed to improve in order to compose a manuscript as such. I wanted to develop a story that many could relate to as well as enjoy.

I was born into a military family which moved around a little during my childhood. Within my travels, I gained an understanding of people. With every new city I lived the people encountered the same problems. Males and females wanted to know where exactly did they stand in a relationship with the opposite sex. I have lived nine lives, nine different places, and all the light skin girls had similar faces.

Many of my theories are crazy and outlandish. In actuality, how much does a person know about the world? Every person lives a separate life with a separate identity that is unknown to most of the world: good and evil, right and wrong. Evolution of the mind and the power of energy and karma are inevitable and cannot be controlled by a person that is sheltered. By sheltered, meaning, many people don't realize that there is a society in which they live.

I was never in a situation growing up that allowed me to disrespect authority. The children of America have become uncontrollable due to their knowledge. Our children have not been given the credit that they desire. They are educated beyond technology, but the system has placed a mental handicap on our youth's growth. They became disengaged in modern day forms of learning. Along with education, the government and private sectors have taken the power away from the adults and placed children on even playing fields with the policies that are in place. If a child is not raised by the village, they don't respect the village.

Society consists of a three-dimensional perception of the world that consists of more than having a 3D perception of objects: the relationship between one's mind, body, soul; royalty, loyalty, respect; life, love, and relationship. That is what make us three-dimensional. Things that happen in our lives are not apart of our doing, but by a greater being. The manifestation of words into existence is what makes us the beings that we are. It is also the reason why history will continue to repeat itself.

In his later work, Freud proposed that the psyche was divided into three parts: ego, super-ego, and identification. Freud discussed his structural mode as an alternative to his previous topographic schema. The three dimensions were simplified to one's conscious, unconscious, preconscious.

Wake up and see reality for what it is. We are at war. We are living in poverty. We are killing each other. We need to wake up before it is too late. One should plant a harvest that will last for many seasons. Break bread until everyone has a piece; for one should never ask the question why or reply when told. It is ok to change rules but stop breaking laws for you will wake a sleeping beast.

Seven Principles of the Story

"The Year of Aphesis"
Black Book Chronicles:
Stop Playing Games

People:

The main character of the story is a nineteen year old young man that's in his first year of college. He was a high school All-American with many awards and honors. He is on a full athletic scholarship for football.

Place:

The original audience is a college campus near the North Carolina-West Virginia border. This is during a time when the economy was good and people had money. Many middle class people where being provided with government assistance and college attendance was high for minority students. Also during this time frame, many rape cases and sexual assault cases were filed due to the growing party scene on college campuses. Clubs were beginning to close earlier placing a limit on how long people could be out late.

Plot:

The main character arrived on campus two days after graduating from high school. During the summer he grows a strong relationship with Amber, and she soon becomes his girlfriend. Once school starts he is introduced into a whole new life. His campus is full of beautiful and intelligent women which he sees as a challenge. Later he meets Casey which causes turmoil. After his separation with Amber, he begins to date again, only to realize he was not happy. While trying to hold on to past relationship his godbrother is killed. He is forced to reevaluate his morals, expectations, and goals.

Point:

The main character was at the point in his life where he was trying to find himself. He was placing people around him in roles that he saw fit, but there was an empty filling inside of him. Being you is in direct correlation with knowing God. Acting is a form of having fun, and having fun is being a fool. You don't want to be a fool all your life.

Principle:

The timeless truth is that people who play the game should know the rules. Read to comprehend. Understand that Loyalty lasts and Honesty is with God. Trust no one because trust has nothing to do with the truth. One can't love another without an attraction, but one can remain loyal when that attraction is gone.

Priorities:

In life, one must first gain control over their physical and mental state. Believe in the intangible, for it is what causes the things we don't see. Understand your position and don't mock those who are struggling. Every process has a struggle. Don't allow money and materialistic objects to cloud your dreams and block your thoughts.

Plan:

Pay attention to the situation at hand. Have as many plans as needed in order to progress. Stop being stuck in situations that society won't let you out of: credit, debt, loans. Stop taking what you don't have and become content with what you do. Money is not your only option.

Reference

Excerpts from the Willie Lynch Speech: (www.thetalkingdrum. com)

Meyer, Glenn E.,Ciccarelli,Saundra K. (2006) 1. Psychology – Textbook. I. Title. Upper Saddle River, New Jersey. Pearson Prentice Hall